CRONIN'S KEY IV

KENNARD'S STORY

N.R. WALKER

BLURB

Kennard and Stas have been enjoying being newly bonded mates, hidden away for the last six months in Stas' cabin, deep in the forests of Northern Russia. When they get a visit from Alec, Cronin, Eiji, and Jodis, Kennard and Stas decide to return to London where they get news of a supernatural disturbance in India.

Excited for a new adventure, the band of friends embark on a journey like they've never seen before. Following a trail of snakes and serpents, they slip through gates into timeless dimensions all over the world, leaving them without their vampire powers. Even Alec is powerless as they follow a trail of gates and doorways to their final destination.

But the bad guy isn't who they think it is, and Kennard will need to draw on his past to save their future. Because history is never what it seems...

COPYRIGHT

Cover Artist: SJ York
Editor: Boho Edits
Publisher: BlueHeart Press
Cronin's Key © 2019 N.R. Walker
First Edition 2019

DEDICATION

For my readers,
who have waited far too long for this...

CRONIN'S KEY IV

KENNARD'S STORY

N.R. WALKER

CHAPTER ONE

"DO you think we should try and get out of bed today?" Kennard asked.

"No." Stas' voice was gruff, warm and delicious in his ear.

Kennard smiled into the mattress and tried to pull himself toward his pillow, a feigned escape attempt, but Stas' huge hand gripped his hip and slid him back into place. Then Stas rolled on top of him, his erection pressing against Kennard's ass. Kennard lifted his hips and spread his legs, giving Stas all the permission he needed as he laughed into the sheet. "It's been six months. I guess one more day won't hurt."

Stas pushed inside him and both men groaned. "We never leave," Stas whispered, his fangs at Kennard's shoulder. "Stay here forever."

Kennard had always doubted the mating bond between vampires. Well, not doubted. He'd never understood it. He'd spent most of his six hundred years alone. He'd had acquaintances and friends and a lot of lovers. Yet his heart had never been moved by anyone. He almost thought it had frozen in his chest when he was changed from human to vampire, because the way he'd seen mated pairs behave was so foreign to him.

But then there was Stas.

As soon as he'd seen him, he knew. The melancholy that had settled over him in the months before, like a mist, had dissolved the moment his eyes fell upon him. His purpose was now clear. This huge, hulking Russian vampire was his.

They'd been holed up in Stas' cabin in Lithuania at first, barely leaving each other's embrace for a minute. Then they'd driven Stas' truck to one of his cabins in some far-off Russian forest and hadn't left each other's side, or their bed. Except to feed, which hadn't been anywhere near as often as it probably should've been, because they seemed to feed off each other. Energy, blood, love. Sex. So much sex, yet nowhere near enough. They'd barely stopped long enough for important conversations. Stas had managed to give some of his history, Kennard even less so.

The desire, the bone-deep need to be with Stas, to have him inside him, to be one with him was so profound it was dizzying. Kennard used to roll his eyes at newly fated mates. They used to make him sick. Now he wanted nothing more.

"You are everything," Stas whispered. He ran his hand through Kennard's hair, messing it up even further, kissing his head. "My everything."

Kennard rolled his hips and pressed his forehead into the mattress, arching his back. "*I ty moy*," Kennard murmured.

And you are mine.

Stas always reacted when Kennard spoke Russian. Especially in bed. He growled into the back of Kennard's neck and sunk his fangs into Kennard's shoulder while he thrust deeper inside him, and Kennard's whole body sang.

Every cell, every fiber of his being.

And afterwards, when Stas had wrung Kennard of every ounce of pleasure, they lay in bed in each other's arms.

"I might even try turning on that old radio set today," Kennard said. "If the batteries work."

Stas laughed. "You said yesterday. And last week."

Kennard laughed into his chest, Stas' chest hair tickling his face, but lovely and soft and warm. "I've lost all track of days."

"I think is March," Stas said with a chuckle.

Kennard found his broken English adorable, and he hummed happily. "Sounds about right."

Stas ran his wide hands over Kennard's slender form, over his pointed hip, up his spine. He was literally twice Kennard's size. Stas had a masculine build, short, dark-brown hair, blue eyes, and a square jaw. Broad shoulders, huge hands. Everything about him screamed man. Whereas Kennard was fine-featured with pretty, boyish looks and white-blond hair. Stas was a loner, his home in the Russian wilds, in a basic cabin with no electricity or running water, and Kennard was a social guy who lived in an expensive apartment with every conceivable technology and thrived in the London nightlife. Opposites in every way, yet one perfectly complemented the other. "Do you wish to feed?" Stas asked.

Kennard considered it and took stock of his body, his baser need to feed. "No," he said simply. "I don't need anything but you right now. What about you?"

But Stas didn't answer. He cocked his head and he frowned. "Hear that?"

It took Kennard a second to shake his mind of his post-coital haze, but then, yes, he could. "Someone is coming? In this weather?" It was snowing. The entire forest was under a blanket of white.

Stas sat up on the bed and pulled on some jeans. "Is human."

"Can you read their mind? Do you know who they are?"

Stas froze and turned back to Kennard, who was still sprawled naked on the bed. "No. I not hear them." He frowned. "How can I not hear them?"

Kennard sat up then. "I don't know."

Stas' cabin was isolated, deep in some Northern Russian forest. It was old, built a few hundred years ago. A simple A-frame log cabin with a bedroom loft on the mezzanine and a small living room on the ground floor, an unused kitchen, and an old-fashioned bathtub they needed to heat water for. It was positively prehistoric compared to Kennard's apartment in London, but it was all Stas had ever needed. He'd relished in the isolation, a reprieve from his vampiric ability to hear the minds of those around him.

The driveway to the cabin was long and overgrown; the cabin couldn't be seen from the road, especially in winter. And most human drivers who passed by—of which there were few—didn't know it was a driveway at all.

Stas had told Kennard he knew humans ignored his driveway because Stas could hear their thoughts. Except he hadn't *heard* a thing since Alec had blocked Stas' mind when they were in the pits under Moscow and...

"Have you heard anything since Moscow and Pennsylvania?" Kennard asked.

Stas seemed confused. "I don't know. I think no. The

campers at lake we found were sleeping, and I focus on you so much, I not notice."

That was true. They'd only fed once, when some foolish hunters camped out by the lake and drank far too much homemade vodka. It was the first time he and Stas had fed together, and well... it had been a feed and fuck fest. Kennard wasn't surprised Stas was so distracted. The memory made him flush. "Well," Kennard said, slipping on a robe. It belonged to Stas, and it swam on Kennard—it was far from his usual stylish garb—but he didn't care. "Let's deal with this human first. See if you can hear anything when you speak to him."

Kennard wasn't sure of the science behind mind reading or how any vampire talent worked, for that matter, but he gave Stas a smile he hoped was a comfort.

A black van came into view, driving slowly, clearly very unsure or lost. It was getting dark and the van's headlights cast a yellow light across the snow. It pulled to a stop, and after a moment, a man exited the vehicle. He slid back the side door and pulled out a large bouquet of flowers. Not just any flowers, but white stargazer lilies.

Funeral lilies.

Kennard burst out laughing, dashed down the stairs, and opened the door. The porch cover was deep enough so no sunlight could reach the front door—not that Northern Russia saw much sunshine—and the delivery man smiled at first. Then upon closer inspection, as though realizing Kennard wasn't exactly human, or perhaps he felt the danger, that cold shiver of fear from being so close to evil, the man's smile disappeared and he stumbled closer to the door. He mumbled something in Russian that Kennard couldn't quite work out—huge payment, middle of nowhere?—but he handed over the large bouquet and staggered back, waving as he climbed into his van before he sped back down the driveway.

Kennard spun inside, twirling like a dancer, and laughed as he held out the flowers. "Well, at least we know what day it is."

Stas was clearly confused. "What?"

"It's March twenty-fourth."

"What is the significance of this date to you?" Stas asked. "And who sent you flowers? Who even knows where we are?"

Kennard flitted over to his big protective lump of a mate, leaned up on his toes, and kissed him. "March twenty-fourth is a dark, dark day in England's history. A day of mourning, really."

Stas was immediately concerned and angry, even. "What is it? What happened to hurt you like this? I will find them!"

Kennard chuckled. "Nothing like that, my love. Cronin sends me flowers on March twenty-fourth, every year, to commemorate the union of the crowns." Kennard frowned and sighed loudly. "A dark, dark day indeed."

Stas cupped Kennard's face. "What is this union of crowns? I not understand."

Kennard shook his head sadly. "It was when a damn Scot became King of England."

Stas blinked, then more confusion etched his brow. "What?"

"In 1603, when the King of Scotland became King of England." Kennard sniffed. "Cronin never lets me forget it. He sends me funeral flowers every year. I'd say Alec knows where we are."

Stas stared at him for a beat, then burst out laughing. "Oh, my Kennard, you scared me!"

Kennard kissed him again, this time with smiling lips. "I'm sorry, my love. It's a little joke between Cronin and myself. We have known each other a long time."

Stas picked up an old jar, blew the dust off it, and poured some water into it. Kennard slotted the bouquet into the jar and they set it on the table. Kennard smiled at how it brightened the room, and he took Stas' hand and pulled him into a hug.

"I should call them," Kennard said. "They're probably wondering how we're getting on. Though, if I can even find my phone, it'll be out of charge. I'll have to start the truck and charge it there."

Stas frowned. "My house bothers you," he mumbled. "Old and far away."

"No." Kennard kissed him. "I like being here with you. This house is perfect for you in every way."

"But not for you..."

"Wherever you are is perfect for me." Kennard put his hands to Stas' face and made him look into his eyes. "Wherever you are is my home, okay? Please don't be sad. When you are sad, it makes me sad."

Stas gave him a smile. "I don't want my Kennard to be sad. Not even on day when a Scot became King of England."

Kennard laughed and kissed him again. "I best go try and find my phone."

"I will light fire for you," he said with a nod. "Make house warm and we have bath."

Kennard hummed at the thought. It was an old cast iron tub that fit them both perfectly. "Yes, please."

Stas planted a sound kiss on Kennard's lips, then set off to rekindle the fire. Kennard darted up the stairs and found his pants. He pulled them on, then threw the robe on the bed in favor of one of Stas' old plaid shirts. It was soft and smelled of pine and earth and everything that Stas smelled like. Kennard pulled on his expensive designer boots that had been kicked into the corner some months ago—the last time he'd worn clothes—and found his jacket in a crumpled heap. He located his phone, which he hadn't even thought of since he'd laid eyes on Stas, and yes, it was completely dead.

He took the stairs back to the living room. "Um, just had a thought... no charger cable."

"Let me look," Stas said. He went to the kitchen drawers and began to rifle through them. He held up one cord. "Is this it?"

It was for a different phone, quite a few years old. "No." Then he saw that Stas had a drawer full of odds and ends. It made him laugh. "You have a junk drawer?"

"Junk?" Stas asked. "Not junk. Might use one day. I find these things on the people... On the bodies of the... in their backpacks or coats." He made a face.

Oh. The personal belongings of his meals.

"Resourceful," Kennard said. He could hardly judge. Taking the rings or gold coins from his meals was how he began to accrue his wealth in the 1600s.

Stas pulled out another cord, staring at it oddly. "This one look new?"

"Yes!" Kennard took the cord and rewarded Stas with a kiss on the cheek. "You're a life saver."

"Well, no. The guy who cord belong to would think not."

Kennard laughed and tweaked Stas' cheek. "Don't get me thinking about you with your mouth on another man's neck." Then he skipped to the door.

"Kennard," Stas called out, stopping him. He threw him the key to the truck. "Need this."

"Thank you, my love."

Kennard flitted down the porch steps. It was darker now, the sun was long gone behind the trees and clouds, and the moon gave the snow a blue and silver hue. He crossed to the garage, feeling every step away from Stas in his heart.

Surely he could walk across the yard without missing him? Surely he could spend five minutes apart from him...

The ache deepened, sharpened. He climbed into the truck, turned on the ignition, and after a bit of a cough and splutter, the truck started. He plugged the USB port into the charger, thankful Stas had a newish truck. Probably an acquisition from an unsuspecting camper in the forest...

The phone beeped with life, though it took a few long seconds for the home screen to appear. A few long, too-far-from-Stas seconds. He pushed the heel of his hand against his chest just as the passenger door opened and Stas climbed in. The relief was immediate. "You feel that too?" Stas asked, rubbing against his chest. "Like knife?"

Kennard nodded. "I did. I feel better now though." He smiled at him, taken aback by Stas' rugged good looks. "You're very handsome in the moonlight."

Stas' loud laughter scared some birds out of a nearby tree, but he leaned across and took hold of Kennard's face. "You are most beautiful man. *Takaya krasivaya*. Skin so fair, pinkest lips, and eyes blue as the sky. Make my heart sing."

Kennard drew his bottom lip between his teeth. "You make my heart sing too."

Through everything they'd done together, joining in all the ways imaginable, Kennard could show Stas how he felt, for words were never enough. They were mates. They were fated; there was no stronger bond. Yet *love* seemed inadequate. Kennard needed a stronger word.

"*Dusha moya*," Kennard said. "Is that the right words?"

"My soul," Stas said, with a slight nod. His eyes filled with a depth that warmed Kennard's heart. "Perfect."

Kennard's phone beeped in his hand, startling them both. And then it continued to beep. Missed calls, messages unending. The London coven, his coven. His manager at the club, his club. His banker, his real estate agent.

"You are missed," Stas said sadly. "In your London."

Kennard sighed. "Apparently." But then he looked up at Stas and gave him a smile. "Let's make this phone call; then we can go inside and you can have me in front of the fire, and in the bath, and wherever else you want..."

THE HIGHWAY OPENED up before them in the evening moonlight, and Alec pulled the sports car to the shoulder of the road. They had "borrowed" a Lamborghini from a drug cartel kingpin in Kazakhstan, who couldn't exactly report it stolen. Well, he couldn't very well report that it had literally disappeared into thin air in front of him. Alec had simply pictured it in his mind and transported it to where he, Cronin, Jodis, and Eiji stood on the side of the highway on the vast plains south of Zhezkazgan.

Alec had driven the car first, as if it were part of the road, out of the city onto the very remote, very flat highway. The car handled like a dream, as its price tag suggested it should. He loved the gentle power of the engine and the speed, and he wanted to drive it for hours. But he had promised driving lessons, and so here they were, on one of the remotest highways on the planet.

It was Cronin's turn first, much to Eiji's annoyance. "That's favoritism," he said from the backseat, pouting with his arms crossed.

Jodis sat beside him and patted his knee. "Patience."

Cronin had never had the need to drive. He could leap to any destination, anywhere in the world, any time he wanted. He had as much need for driving a car as he would for flying in a plane. But his grin as he slid behind the wheel told Alec all he needed to know. This wasn't about necessity or convenience. This was about fun.

"I watched what you did," he said, searching the dash and testing the foot pedals. "Though I fear to look like a fool in my first attempt."

I can transfer a driving manual directly into your subcortex, if you'd like, he said directly into Cronin's mind. *Eiji doesn't have to know.*

Cronin fought a smile and gave him the slightest nod.

Alec grinned at him.

Using his talent to search texts from libraries in far-off places or the internet, he scanned a driver's manual, then the instruction manual for this car model. Then he simply transferred the information into Cronin's mind.

Cronin blinked a few times as he took in the information and processed it. Then he grinned and slowly pumped the gas, and smoothly veered the car onto the road. He changed gears flawlessly and took the Lamborghini to top speed like a pro. He handled the car just as Alec knew he would. Incredibly fast, exceptionally well, but without recklessness or irresponsibility. He grinned the entire time, as did Jodis.

Eiji hollered in the backseat. "My turn, my turn!"

Cronin pulled the car over, bringing them to a perfect,

textbook stop. He turned in his seat and grinned at Jodis. "Ladies first."

Jodis clapped, but Eiji's smile died slowly and painfully. "How is this fair? How? Jodis, my love, you can't do this to me!"

But she was already in the front seat, and Cronin slid in beside Eiji, whose pout and crossed arms were hilarious, making Alec laugh.

"Not funny."

Oh, it's funny as hell.

Eiji glowered at him. *I liked you better when you were pretending not to have powers.*

Alec only laughed some more. Then he spoke directly into Jodis' mind. *I can show you how to drive, but don't tell Eiji.*

She grinned and pretended to adjust something on the dash. "Okay."

So he gave her the same information he'd given Cronin, and the next second, she'd shifted to first gear, dropped the clutch, and spun them back onto the highway. Jodis took them from naught to sixty in 0.4 seconds.

"Holy shit," Alec said, gripping the side of his door. The scenery, the vast desert flatness and snow-covered mountains in the distance screamed past his window, and all he could do was laugh.

Jodis slowed the car, and at first Alec thought she may have been pulling up to a stop, but then he saw in her mind what she planned to do. He braced himself on the door and the dashboard just as Jodis spun the car, dropped the clutch, pulled on the handbrake, and drifted them to a stop facing the way they'd come. It was perfect.

Alec let out a low breath. "Dominic Toretto would be proud," he said.

Jodis turned to him, a smug smile on her beautiful face. "Who's that?"

Alec shrugged. "Never mind." Then he turned to the backseat. Cronin was still grinning, and Eiji looked at Alec, hopeful. "Okay, Eiji, it's—"

Eiji was already out of the car and waiting at the driver's door. He peered into the window and tapped on the glass. "My turn, my turn."

Alec laughed, and he climbed into the back with Cronin, and Jodis took the front passenger seat. "Just don't kill us," Alec said.

"Are you sure this is safe?" Cronin asked.

"No," Alec answered. "I'm certain it's not, but I promised him."

Eiji buckled in his seatbelt, put two hands on the steering wheel, and grinned. "How do I make it go?"

Oh, dear God. "Okay, first put your foot on the clutch."

Eiji put his foot on the brake.

Alec held in a laugh. "No, the other one."

Eiji tried the gas this time.

Alec shook his head. "No, the other *other* one."

"Oh great," Jodis mumbled. "We're going to die."

Eiji looked at them in turn. "How did you know what to do so fast? You drive like Grand Theft Auto!"

"I don't know," Cronin lied. "It just came naturally."

Jodis laughed and Eiji stared at her. "I can't lie to him!" Then she gave a nod to Alec. "Show him, please. I can't take this anymore."

"Okay Eij," Alec said. "Brace yourself for an info-dump." Then Alec gave Eiji the driving manuals he'd given the other two.

Eiji blinked a few times. "I knew Cronin cheated!" he said. Alec could see in his mind how Eiji processed the information, then he looked at Alec and his perma-smile became a toothy grin, which really should have scared Alec, but all he could do was laugh.

Eiji restarted the car, stepped on the clutch, shifted the car into gear, and pulled out onto the road... at two miles per hour. Then he increased his speed to eight miles per hour and held onto the wheel with both hands, peering over the dashboard. A butterfly flittered past the window at a faster speed than them.

Alec shot Cronin a disbelieving look. *We just got over-taken by a bug*, Alec whispered into Cronin's mind.

Cronin had to bury his face in his hands as he shook with silent laughter, and Jodis glanced back at them and coughed to cover a giggle.

"What's so funny?" Eiji asked, not taking his eyes off the road.

"Nothing, my dear," Jodis answered. "You're doing great." She reached over and gently traced her finger through his long black hair, tucking it behind his ear.

"Don't touch me, Jodis," he said. "Trying to concentrate." He leaned in closer to the steering wheel and squinted out the windshield at the road ahead.

"Perhaps we could try second gear," Cronin said with a chuckle.

Alec bit back a bubble of laughter. He could literally walk faster. But before he could reply, Cronin's phone beeped with a message.

Flower delivery confirmation.

"Ah, Kennard's flowers have arrived," he said with an amused smirk.

"Perhaps we could pay them a visit," Jodis said. "We're not far from Russia."

"True," Cronin answered. "Though at this speed, it would take us a month."

"I'm driving fast!" Eiji barked.

Cronin grinned. "Alec, *m'cridhe*, perhaps you could download a dictionary into Eiji's mind with an emphasis on the definition of fast."

Eiji spun in his seat to glare at Cronin but swerved onto the wrong side of the road. Jodis reached over and corrected the wheel. "Perhaps Alec can leap us to Kennard," she said with a pointed glance at Eiji. "I think I've had enough driving for one day."

"But I just got started," Eiji argued. He was now back to five miles per hour.

Alec laughed. "Well, I think we'll need to give Kennard and Stas some notice. They... they've been... nonstop." He cringed. He'd only pried into Kennard's mind a few times, for a millisecond at best, but it was enough. He didn't mean to intentionally snoop, but sometimes if he wasn't concentrating, all Alec had to do was think of a person and he could see directly into their minds. He knew exactly what Stas was doing to Kennard before Alec could snap back into his own head. "And they've been doing it well, I might add."

Cronin laughed. "Ah, newly fated mates." He took Alec's hand. "Such a wonderful thing."

Alec leaned in and kissed him with smiling lips. "It really is." Then he grinned at him. "Ever made out with someone in the backseat of a car?"

"Please," Eiji whined. "I'm trying to concentrate. You distract me with your pheromones."

Alec laughed. "Never mind. Cronin's getting a phone call in three, two, one..."

Right on cue, Cronin's phone rang. He read the name on the screen and answered with a smile. "Kennard!"

CHAPTER TWO

"GIVE US FIVE MINUTES," Kennard said before clicking off the call. "Stas, my love. We need to be presentable for company."

Stas stared at him. "Company. In five minutes?"

Kennard straightened up some cushions. "Yes. Cronin, Alec, Jodis, and Eiji."

"How they get here? Driving?" He peered out the window toward the driveway.

"Uh, no. They'll be leaping here."

Stas frowned and looked around, then looked down at himself. "I should get dressed..."

Kennard laughed, flitted over to kiss him, before going on to tidy up a little. Not that there was much to do. Granted, the cabin was small, but the open fire ensured a fine layer of dust covered most surfaces. The couch was old, the carpet rug was old—Stas was almost eight hundred years old, Kennard allowed. Most things he owned were old.

And the smell of sex permeated everything from the loft bedroom down to the floorboards... well, there was nothing they could do about that. But Kennard happily plumped the cushion and dusted, tidying, straightening.

Stas came thudding back down the stairs wearing his usual attire of hiking boots, jeans, and a plaid flannel long-sleeved shirt. If Kennard had seen him walking down a London street, he'd probably have called the look lumber-sexual, but here in a log cabin, deep in the woods of the Russian wilds, it was just... hot.

His rugged wardrobe matched his rugged handsome-ness perfectly. He was a big man with broad shoulders and chest, huge biceps, a thick neck, and a square jaw. He'd told Kennard that when he was human, he'd led men in battle, and Kennard could believe it. He was a human tank. But then in the spring of 1223, the Mongol coven had invaded Kievan Rus, and Stas, even as huge as he was, was no match for a swarm of vampires.

They came in the dead of night, slaying and feeding as they went, and Stas was left for dead. Only he didn't die... He awoke to a burning pain that Kennard knew all too well. And when the pain finally withered away, Stas was left with a cacophony of voices in his head. At first, he thought the pain had sent him mad, until he realized what it was. And he found over time, the only reprieve he could get from the minds of others was distance and solitude.

Kennard took Stas' hand. "Are you comfortable with visitors?" he asked. "They won't be here for long."

"I am fine," Stas said, though Kennard could see he was not.

"You don't have to pretend with me, my love," Kennard said softly. "I can feel your anxiety, remember?"

Stas let out a sigh. "I worry, that is all. For the voices."

"You still can't hear me?"

Stas shook his head slowly. "I not know if that is good or

bad thing. I hate the voices, but maybe yours... maybe yours be not so bad."

Kennard laughed just as four vampires appeared in their living room. It was always a little startling, but as soon as Kennard saw his friends, he smiled. "Cronin," he said, letting go of Stas' hand so he could greet them all properly. He hugged them all, quite taken aback by how much he'd missed them. "Thank you for coming. I wasn't expecting you all, but Eiji and Jodis, it's always a pleasure." Then he looked at Alec and purred. "And you, dear Alec. Handsome as ever."

Stas growled from behind him, and Kennard turned to him and laughed. He dashed back to his side, linking their arms and wrapping his body against Stas like a cat. "You guys remember my Stas?"

"Yes, of course," Cronin said, extending his hand. "A pleasure to meet you under less stressful circumstances." They shook hands, and Cronin added, "And ignore how Kennard and Alec are together. Harmless flirts, both of them."

Kennard noticed Alec hadn't taken his eyes off him. "Kennard, you look..."

Kennard looked down at his outfit. "Rugged lumbersexual?"

Eiji snorted. "Rugged what? Please excuse us, but I don't want to know what you guys do with wood." He put his hand up. "Not my business."

Jodis laughed. "Not lumber sexual... Never mind. I'll explain when you're older."

Alec grinned but shook his head at Kennard. "You look happy, my friend. Incredibly happy."

Cronin and Jodis nodded. "True."

Eiji was still confused, squinting at Jodis. "What do you mean when I'm older? I'm the oldest one here."

Jodis laughed and smiled fondly at Stas. "You have a beautiful home. Thank you for having us."

Stas gave a hard nod. "You are welcome. It is good to see you again. Thank you for coming when my Kennard ask you."

My Kennard...

Kennard resisted swooning and instead smiled up at him, happy Stas was making an effort with his friends.

"About that," Alec started. "Kennard, you wanted to see me?"

"Well, yes," Kennard said. "You remember how, when we were in those terrible pits in Moscow with those dreadful Zoan creatures, you shielded Stas' mind? Well, he still can't hear any thoughts, and I was wondering if you know why that is. Because you relinquished your powers, did you not?"

A slow smile spread across Alec's face. "I was wondering how long it was going to take for you guys to realize."

"Realize what?" Kennard asked with a smirk. "That Stas didn't have his power, or that you still had yours?"

Now Alec laughed. "Yes, I still have my powers. The elders' council know, of course. But we thought it wouldn't hurt for everyone else to think I didn't."

"Less threat to Alec that way," Cronin said. "The thing with power is that someone else always thinks they're more entitled to it."

"And if a Transfer were to take his powers..." Jodis added.

Kennard nodded. "Fair enough. And just so you all

know, we did notice Stas couldn't hear minds before now." He cleared his throat. "We just couldn't..."

"Bring yourselves to stop doing what you were doing?" Alec said with a grin. "We all know what it's like to be newly bonded mates."

"Yes, well..." Kennard couldn't even deny it.

"You really do look happy," Cronin said quietly. "Happier than I've ever seen you."

Alec, Eiji, and Jodis all nodded in agreement. "Can I show you both something?" Alec asked. "In your minds?"

Kennard was used to Alec's talent and Stas had seen Alec's mind tricks when they first met in Moscow, so they both nodded. Then in Kennard's mind, he saw two pictures. Like photographs, only snapshots of memories. The first picture was of Kennard in his London apartment when Alec and Cronin had visited him and he'd admitted to being unhappy. He'd spent months in a haze of melancholy and loneliness. His outfit was immaculate: black Italian leather coat and boots, designer pants, his hair coiffed up to a flawless style. And immeasurable sadness on his face, dull eyes and a forced smile.

And the second picture was of him standing there, right that moment, pressed up against Stas. He wore one of Stas' old oversized lumberjack shirts, and his blond hair was in flattened disarray, but it wasn't his clothes or hair that were noticeably different. It was his face. His eyes had life and light, his smile was pure joy. They were right; he looked so goddamned happy. Kennard laughed and lifted his right foot, pointing his toe. "Still have the Armani boots though."

Stas turned to him, concerned. He put his huge hand to Kennard's face. "Why you look so sad? In first memory, my Kennard, you were sad."

Kennard smiled at him. "I was. Because I hadn't met

you yet." Then Kennard kissed the palm of Stas' hand and gave Alec a smile. "Thank you for showing me that."

"You're welcome," Alec replied. He gave Stas a nod. "I apologize for shielding your talent without your consent. I should have been truthful, and I am sorry for any confusion or discomfort."

Stas swallowed hard; then he looked at each of them, his gaze lingering on Kennard before he looked back to Alec. "I not know if I want it back. For first time in almost eight centuries, I have peace. I lock myself away to not hear the voices so I am used to silence"—he waved his hand toward the wall—"out here in forest. But you stand here now and I not hear anything." His eyes drew back to Kennard. "I not hear my Kennard at all..."

Alec frowned. "You don't want your talent back?"

Every pair of eyes drew to Stas, and he slowly shook his head, but then he looked at Kennard, as though he were torn. "I not know. I would say no, but now if danger comes and I not have mind-hearing, how can I warn my Kennard and keep him safe?"

Kennard's heart squeezed. "Oh, you big oaf. Do this for you. Not for me," he said, though he knew as soon as he said it, it wasn't fair. Because a vampire would do anything for their mate, it was unfair of Kennard to tell him not to.

Stas' brow furrowed. "What is oaf?"

Shit.

"An oaf is..." Kennard was stuck. He couldn't lie to Stas.

But Alec could. "An oaf is an affectionate term..."

"For a loved one," Cronin added.

"Who is a big lump like you," Eiji added with a smile. Everyone turned to glare at Eiji. "What?" he cried.

"Kennard calls you an oaf because you are big and lovable," Jodis smoothed over.

Stas pouted and Kennard wrapped his arms around him and chuckled. "He is, indeed."

"Ah," Cronin said, changing the subject. "I see your flowers were delivered."

"Yes, which prompted my phone call," Kennard replied. "I take it Alec used his endless talents to pluck the delivery address out of thin air."

Alec gave him a smile. "Yes. We had to confirm the address several times. The driver didn't believe us."

"My condolences, anyway," Cronin said with a smirk. "I know this is a dark day for you."

Kennard sighed dramatically. "A travesty is what it was."

Alec laughed, and he glanced at Stas. He must have seen something in his mind because he said, "You know Kennard is a staunch monarchist. Hates the Scottish. And the Irish."

"And the French," Kennard added with a sniff. "Actually, there's quite a list."

Everyone laughed, and even Stas smiled. "But not Russia."

Kennard almost purred. "Oh, no. I'm rather fond of Russia."

Stas ran his hand down Kennard's back and pulled him in close for a bruising kiss, as though he'd forgotten they had company.

Alec cleared his throat and shut his eyes tight. "Wow, okay. Uh, that was a visual I wasn't prepared for."

Kennard laughed loudly, snuggling into Stas' side. "He's impressive, is he not?"

Everyone in the room smiled, and Stas took a deep breath. "If I can ask for favor," he said. "Can please you leap us to Kennard's London? He tells me he does not miss it, but I know he does."

"I am happy here," Kennard argued. "You saw those memories of me; you saw how happy I am."

"Yes," Stas said, gently moving a strand of hair off Kennard's forehead. "I want to see where you are from. Your home, your club, your coven."

And there it was. The word that sent a pang through Kennard's heart. A pang that Stas no doubt felt as well.

Stas smiled. "See? You must return. As elder, you've been gone too long."

Kennard sighed and pressed his forehead to Stas' chest, but he nodded. "I know."

Stas enveloped Kennard in his strong arms, gentle and loving. "We go to your England, yes?"

Kennard nodded and looked over at Alec and Cronin from behind Stas' embrace. "Would either of you gentlemen, with the convenience of leaping, mind dropping us off in my apartment?"

"It'd be my pleasure," Cronin answered.

"Or I could drive!" Eiji cried.

"No!" Alec and Jodis replied in unison.

Kennard chuckled and raised an eyebrow at Eiji. "You? Drove a car?"

"Like the wind," Eiji said, panning his hand out over the horizon.

"If the wind was blowing at one mile an hour," Alec added with a laugh. "And yes, I gave them lessons."

I take it Eiji's lesson didn't go well? Kennard asked Alec in his mind.

Alec grinned. *Like a sloth in molasses.*

Kennard laughed into Stas' chest, then looked up at him. "Are you ready to go?"

"Whenever you are," he murmured before giving Kennard a quick kiss. But as soon as their mouths met, Kennard immediately wanted more.

"Okay, okay," Alec said, putting his hand up in a stop motion. "Jesus. We need to get these guys back to London where there's privacy and hopefully some soundproofing."

Kennard laughed, and in the blink of an eye, they were gone.

KENNARD'S APARTMENT WAS, of course, just how he'd left it. Stylishly minimalistic, dark marble floors, white walls, black leather sofas. It had been his home for over a decade, refurbished to suit his style. And budget.

He immediately missed the rustic warmth of Stas' cabin, the comfort in the closeness. Stas looked around, then nodded toward the glass wall that gave an incredible view of the London skyline. "The window...," Stas said. Even though it was dark outside, vampires generally avoided windows.

"Special filtered glass," Kennard explained. "Blocks out the UV light."

Stas nodded, but then he grimaced at the same time Kennard put a hand to his throat. Suddenly surrounded by a few million beating hearts reminded him of other needs. "I think I need to feed," Kennard whispered.

"You've been away from humans for too long. You can only live off each other for so long. Believe me, I know," Alec said. "Go, take Stas out for a London meal."

"Will you be here when we get back?" Kennard asked. "We shan't be long."

"Of course we will," Cronin said.

Kennard looked up at Stas and took his hand. "You've never seen London?"

Stas shook his head. "No."

Kennard pulled him to the door. "Then let me show you my town."

It was ten past two in the morning and Soho, London, was thumping. Kennard couldn't deny he'd missed the sights and sounds of London. The familiar streets and English cars and buildings were a sight for sore eyes. Kennard's excitement ratcheted up a notch as they approached the entrance of his club. The vampires at the door looked twice at Kennard—clearly not used to his flannelette plaid shirt and messy hair—then bowed their heads and opened the doors. "Kennard, so good to see you," one of them said. They looked up to Stas and swallowed hard, clearly intimidated by his size.

"This is Stas," Kennard announced with a smile. "He is my mate. Treat him as you would me."

Both men at the door, Carl and Jason, stared at Kennard then. Not at the announcement of Stas being his mate, Kennard realized. But at his smile. "Yes, sir," Carl said quickly, and Kennard led Stas inside.

The nightclub had two levels of bars and dance floors and a third level of private rooms for invited vampires only, and Kennard's office. As soon as Kennard entered, all the vampires noticed immediately. The humans were oblivious to the whispers and hushed murmurs of the coven leader's return. Kennard leaped up onto the platform, holding onto the column, and raised his other hand. The DJ cut the music and everyone stopped and turned toward him.

"Welcome back," someone called out.

Kennard smiled and he almost swung off the column. "It's good to be back. I apologize for my absence."

Kennard knew they were all suspicious of his smile. The old Kennard rarely smiled, and no one dared speak out of turn. But he was different now. "Next round of drinks is on the house."

Everyone cheered, and Kennard gave the barman a nod before leading Stas up to the third floor. It was empty, as it should have been in Kennard's absence. Kennard closed the door behind Stas and turned around, his arms out. "Well, what do you think?"

Stas looked around the dark room. It was painted dark charcoal, with black furniture, and opulent silver chandeliers and candelabra. "It is gothic," he said.

"Yes, perhaps I chose the décor when I was in a mood," Kennard said.

"Your people, they not know what to make of you," Stas said. "They eye you with caution."

Kennard laughed. "Yes. They're not used to seeing me smile."

Just then, there was a knock at the door.

"Come in," Kennard said pleasantly.

Stephanie entered, unsure, but with more confidence than anyone else probably would have. She balked at his outfit but covered it well. She wore a tight-fitting pantsuit and heels, had sharp brown eyes, and Kennard had never seen her brown hair in anything but a sleek ponytail. She took care of the club whenever Kennard had other business to attend to, and Kennard would probably even dare to call her a friend. "Kennard," she said. "Such a pleasure to have you back."

"I do apologize for not calling," Kennard said. "I've been... busy."

Stephanie glanced at Stas, then back at Kennard with wide eyes. "Your mate?"

Kennard gave Stas a smile. "Stephanie has a talent for sensing someone's intent or their purpose. It's what makes her a great manager."

Stephanie preened at the compliment and further explained, "I can also sense bonds between mated vampires. Only when they're together, I can feel their energies."

"Good," Stas said. "I have talent also, only now I don't..."

Kennard laughed. "Stas can read minds, but he's shielding right now. Nothing like going from the quiet wilds of Russia to the middle of London to make him crazy."

"Good idea," Stephanie said. "I can imagine that'd be quite the adjustment. Being able to shield your talent must be a blessing."

Both Kennard and Stas knew he couldn't shield, but Kennard didn't want to display any weakness on Stas' behalf. He changed the subject. "How is everything downstairs? Everyone behaving themselves?"

"That's what I came up to tell you," she replied. "In your absence, I would act in your best interest, but given you've returned, I'd rather have your input."

"Go on," Kennard urged.

"I've picked up on the intent of one man. He's here looking for prey."

"Vampire?"

"No, human. He has Rohypnol in his pocket. I can smell it."

Kennard smiled. "Brilliant. Please bring him up here. No witnesses. Stas and I need a drink."

Stephanie smiled. "As you wish." She got to the door and paused as if she was about to say something, stopped herself, then thought twice and said it anyway. "You look good, Kennard. You wear happiness well; it suits you." And with that, she slipped out the door.

Kennard rolled his eyes. "I think they'd prefer me to snarl and glower at people. Perhaps my smile scares them," he said with a laugh.

Only Stas didn't smile. He took Kennard's hand, concern etched on his brow. "You will bring human up here for us? To feed? Here?"

Kennard gave a nod. "In my office, but yes." He lifted Stas' hand to his lips and kissed his knuckles. "I do try and only feed upon those who deserve it. And quite frankly, those who intend to drug and assault someone do deserve to die."

Just then, the door opened and Jason, who held security at the front door, led a guy into the room, pushed him forward, and he almost fell but collected himself. Jason turned on his heel and walked out, locking the door behind him, leaving a somewhat bewildered male human alone with Kennard and Stas.

Kennard could smell his fear.

"Come this way," Kennard said smoothly, extending his hand toward his office. "We need to have a little chat."

Stas entered the office first and stood by the desk. "I didn't do nuthin'," the man said. Kennard locked the door behind them, and the man's fear spiked, his heart rate too. His eyes kept going from Kennard to Stas, back to Kennard. "You can't lock me in here. Who do you think you are?"

Kennard smiled. "Let me ask you something," he purred, walking over to him. "You like to pick out a victim. Someone smaller than you, someone who won't fight back. And you drug them to ensure their compliance. Then you do sordid things to them without their consent."

The man shook his head; his fear was now becoming panic. "I don't know..."

Kennard walked forward, backing the man into Stas, who was quick to hold him. Kennard reached into the man's front jeans pocket. It felt intimate, personal, but he took out a small foil blister pack of Rohypnol. The man began to protest, but Kennard held the man's face in his hands and let his fangs drop down. The man's eyes went wide and he struggled between them, but he was no match. Kennard tilted the man's neck and purred to Stas. "You first, my love."

The man kicked and thrashed, but they sandwiched him between them. Stas smiled as his fangs extended, drawing a growl of desire from Kennard. Reacting to the sound, Stas leaned down and bit into the man's neck and drank, and when he pulled back, his lips were tinted with blood.

"Now you, my Kennard."

Kennard bit into the warm flesh and gulped down the first mouthful. The warm, metallic liquid ran down his throat, quenching a primal thirst. Then Stas was joining him, their mouths and lips touching, tongues swirling as they drank together.

Kennard hadn't even noticed that the man had stopped kicking. They drank until the blood was gone, and when they could get no more, Stas pushed the body away and grabbed hold of Kennard, kissing him, devouring his mouth and pressing him against the desk. Kennard groaned when he felt how hard Stas was. He wrapped his legs around Stas and rubbed their erections against each other. But it wasn't enough.

Stas growled, and fisting Kennard's jeans at his hip, he shredded them like paper. Kennard laughed as he lay back on the desk, his legs spread as threads of denim drifted like flurries of snow to the floor. Stas undid his jeans and freed his cock, then in one deep push, he buried himself inside Kennard, both of them groaning, long and loud.

Kennard, with his back arched, his neck strained, had no words for how complete he felt.

He'd always heard that feeding with a mate was incredibly sensual. He could still taste the blood in their kiss, and now he was impaled, joined as one with the man he loved. Every nerve ending, every cell was alight with pleasure, instinct and primal need. He was so turned on, he was so aroused that when Stas reached between them and fisted Kennard's cock, he came.

His orgasm detonated in his entire body. A blinding light bloomed inside him, a pleasure so profound, so encompassing...

Then Stas leaned back and gripped his hips, thrusting in hard before he spilled deep, deep inside him.

Stas collapsed on top of him, and neither of them moved. Kennard didn't think he was capable. "We need to do that again."

Stas laughed, a hearty rumble. "Yes, please. *Vsegda bol'she.*" He looked up at Kennard and Kennard could see Stas' fangs were still out.

Kennard leaned up and ran his tongue over the sharp points. "So hot."

Stas answered with a deep kiss and another thrust of his hips. Kennard moaned, his body arching into Stas, impaled on him still.

And when they were done for a second time, when he was thoroughly had and sated, they lay on the floor, Kennard tracing his fingers through Stas' hair, and Kennard sighed.

"What is matter?" Stas asked.

"Just thinking it's a shame we have to leave right now. I would love nothing more than to stay here another day, another week. A month."

"Why we need to leave now for?" Stas mumbled.

"It'll be getting light outside soon."

Stas jolted up. "Oh. What is time?"

"Five thirty." Stas jumped to his feet and pulled Kennard up. "Uh, slight problem," Kennard said as he looked down at his naked self. "You ripped my jeans."

Stas chuckled, then looked to the bloodless body slumped on the floor. "He not need his anymore."

Kennard laughed, and ten minutes later he and Stas walked out, hand in hand, laughing as they made their way back to Kennard's apartment. Kennard's new jeans were so big they kept falling down, so Stas had Kennard over his shoulder and they were still laughing as they came through his apartment door. "Oh, Cronin, darling," Kennard said, still upside down over Stas' shoulder. "There're some unsightly leftovers on my office floor. Would you be a sweetheart and dispose of it?"

Cronin chuckled from across the room, and it was then Kennard realized they were all transfixed by the television—or more specifically, a golden temple on the television. He leaned up and slid down Stas' body to land on his feet. "What are you all watching?"

Eiji answered with a grin. "There's a temple in India with a mysterious vault that is sealed shut. No one can open it."

Eiji looked far too excited for Kennard's liking, which never ended well, so Kennard looked to Alec. He was sitting with his eyes closed and a serious look of concentration on his face. He opened his eyes and gave Kennard a smirk.

"The ancient Padmanabhaswamy Temple in Southwestern India is sealed closed. Absolutely no way in or out. Hindu priests say that at present, there is no human capable of opening it."

Kennard was almost too scared to ask. "And?"

Eiji's grin widened and he waved his arms around as he spoke. "And the door is huge, and there are two cobra statues who guard it and—"

"Let me guess," Kennard deadpanned. "Like the mummies in Egypt, and like the Terracotta Army in China, and like the stone gargoyles in Paris... they moved all on their own."

"Yes!" Eiji jumped and clapped, making Jodis and Alec laugh.

Kennard sighed dramatically and took Stas' hand. "Stas, my love. Have you ever been to India?"

CHAPTER THREE

"SO, the Scooby-Doo Gang is back together," Kennard said. He smiled at the thought. The thing with living an incredibly long life was that it could get tedious, so a little adventure was always a great distraction. "I have to admit, Alec. All of my five hundred years have never been quite as interesting as in the last few years since I met you."

Cronin reappeared, making Kennard and Stas flinch. He gave Kennard a nod. "My friends in Tanzania said to say thank you."

Alec laughed at what Kennard assumed was an inside joke, and he welcomed Cronin back with a kiss. "Kennard and Stas will come with us to India."

"Excellent," Cronin said. He leaned into Alec, and once upon a time, Kennard would have rolled his eyes at their need to touch each other, but now he understood it. Jodis and Eiji weren't so inclined to be all over each other, but they'd been mated for longer than Kennard had been alive. They were still drawn to one another but they had a better handle on the emotional bond. They could even spend time apart, whereas Kennard couldn't even imagine being in a different room than Stas.

"When do we go?" Eiji asked. "Can we go now?"

"It's still daytime in India," Alec said. "We have a few hours to work out a contingency plan."

"We can take weapons," Eiji said excitedly. "What weapons do we need, Alec? Who is the bad guy and how do we kill them?"

Kennard snorted. "Wasn't your great contingency plan in China just to, and I quote, 'Take a hammer and smash shit up'?"

They laughed, but Stas was more serious. Alec's gaze darted to Stas, and Kennard wondered what Stas was thinking to grab Alec's attention. "What is it, my love?"

Stas gave him a wry smile. "Normally I am the one who reads minds," he said. Then he nodded toward Alec. "I just want to say thanks for what you did in China. My Kennard told me how you kill Khan." Stas looked to all of them, even blushing a little. "Khan's coven was who changed me. My men hold line outside Kiev when the Mongol coven came. Only I survive. I wish I be with you in China to see his end. But thank you for seeing it done."

"You're welcome," Alec said gently. "Though it was Cronin who killed Khan." He gave Cronin a fond smile.

"You're welcome," Cronin added. "And thank you for your help in Moscow, and in Pennsylvania. We couldn't have done it without you."

"The boy," Stas said. "Jorge? Is he happy now?"

Alec smiled and nodded. "Much happier."

Kennard slid his arm around Stas and gave him a squeeze. "My big teddy bear."

Stas blushed at the term of endearment. "Teddy bear? I thought I was oaf."

Jodis looked Kennard up and down. "Uh, nice jeans," she said with a smile.

Kennard looked down at the too-big, too-cheap denim jeans he was holding up at the waist. "Well, yes. I had a... wardrobe malfunction. I should get changed."

Stas blushed some more and Alec snorted. "That was a memory I didn't need to see, but thanks."

Kennard laughed and dragged Stas by the hand to the hall. "If we have a few hours, we might um... get changed. And showered, and... um, these walls aren't exactly sound-proofed, so you might want to turn the television up."

He heard them laugh as he closed his bedroom door, threw his arms around Stas' neck, and climbed up his body, wrapping his legs around his waist. "Any ideas how we can fill in a few hours?"

"You still not have enough?" Stas whispered.

"Never enough. I could have you inside me every minute of every day."

Someone in the living room cleared their throat and the volume of the television went up, making Kennard laugh.

"They hear us," Stas whispered as he made a face.

Kennard didn't care if all of London heard him, but Stas was clearly not so comfortable. Kennard had spent centuries surrounded by millions of people, whereas Stas had spent just as long in solitude. So he unwrapped himself and jumped down, taking Stas' hand and pulling him toward the adjoining private bathroom. "Then let us shower together."

Stas scoffed. "I know how that will end."

Kennard laughed, but when he turned around to say something, he saw that Stas was looking around his bedroom. Kennard stopped walking and let Stas take it all in. The room was huge with tall ceilings, black marble floor, white walls, a huge black bed, black dresser, and a silver-gilded mirror. The furniture was expensive, luxurious, and completely over the top. "Some might call it French deco, but I don't like to admit that," Kennard said with a wink.

But Stas was now staring at the black chandelier that hung over the center of the room. He didn't say anything—he didn't need to. Kennard was sure where his mind had gone. "I know it's a bit extravagant. I should totally redo the whole apartment. It's about time I redecorated anyway."

"No. It is... very nice. Like palace." Stas looked to Kennard then, his eyes wide. "You have good taste."

Kennard chuckled, though more to hide his embarrassment. He felt a little foolish for such opulence. "Well, yes. I have impeccable taste. That is true." The truth was, his bedroom wasn't even the worst of it. "Have a look at this."

He walked to a closed door, opened it, and flipped the lights on. His wardrobe was just as big as his bedroom. Black cabinetry with specialized backlighting showed all the clothes were hanging immaculately, organized rows of shoes and boots, display counters of watches and cufflinks. Gucci, YSL, Versace, Dolce & Gabbana, Armani, Tiffany; the list was endless, expensive, and elite.

Stas stood there, staring, speechless.

"It's probably a little much," Kennard mumbled. He could see now that he'd spent years overcompensating for his loneliness with clothes and material things. "I thought I could buy happiness," he whispered, running his finger down the sleeve of a four-thousand-dollar jacket he'd never worn.

Stas pulled him in for a hug, and only when Kennard snuggled into his chest did Stas begin to purr. "You are happy now, yes?"

"Yes. Happiness isn't money or things. It's here," Kennard murmured, kissing Stas' chest, over his heart. "It's you, and my friends out there." Kennard looked up at Stas' face. "I didn't know it could be like this."

"Not me either," Stas said. "I spend long time alone. Then there is you and I not be sad now too."

"We make a good pair," Kennard mused.

"I like your house," Stas said.

This surprised Kennard. "You do?"

Stas nodded, smiling. "Very much." He looked back over his shoulder. "Your view, your things. And I would very much like to try your bed."

Kennard laughed and bopped his dainty finger on the tip of Stas' nose. "I like the way you think, my love. But if you like my view, my house, and my wardrobe, just wait until you see the shower."

Kennard dragged him into the bathroom, which was half the size of the wardrobe. Stas gawped at the lavish Italian marble, at the custom designed fittings. "Is bigger than my whole house!"

Kennard laughed. "Close your mouth, my love. Or I'll find something to fill it with." Kennard pulled off his boots and tossed them back toward the wardrobe, then pulled off his shirt and let his too-big jeans fall to the floor. He walked into the shower and started the water. The hot water felt amazing, and it elicited a low moan.

That made Stas move. He ripped his clothes off and joined Kennard, testing the hot water, the expensive body washes and shampoos, then testing the softest towels money could buy, then they tested Kennard's bed.

Afterwards, Stas lay on his back smiling at the black chandelier, and Kennard was firmly entwined at his side, his head on Stas' chest. "I like your shower, very much," Stas murmured. "What are those spouts called?"

"Dual jets."

"I like dual jets very much."

Kennard chuckled. "I like your cast iron tub. I like your cabin."

"You do?"

Kennard propped his head up on his hand so he could see Stas' eyes. "Yes."

There was a knock on their bedroom door. "Incoming," Alec called out from the hallway. Then, a pile of neatly folded clothes appeared on the end of the bed. "For Stas."

"Thank you, darling," Kennard called out. Then he sighed. "Well, my love. Sounds like plans have been made. Shall we go and see what adventures await?"

They sat up and Stas pulled the pile of clothes over. "He can just make clothes appear in thin air?"

Kennard took the plaid shirt on top and held it up. "And he has great taste, I might add."

"I chose that," Jodis answered from the living room. "You're welcome. Alec was going to get the red, but I went with the blue."

Kennard slipped out of bed and went to his wardrobe. He chose a pair of black YSL jeans, a sheer gray Armani T-shirt, his favorite boots, and he walked out to find Stas pulling on his hiking boots. He took one look at Kennard and gasped. "My Kennard, you are..." He put his hand over his heart. "You take my breath."

Kennard's chest bloomed with warmth and love. "And you are so very handsome."

Stas stood to his full height and pressed his shirt down. "You like?"

"The blue matches your eyes perfectly," Kennard answered.

"Told you," Jodis mumbled from the living room.

"His other shirt was red," Alec hissed back.

Kennard laughed and, taking Stas' hand, led him back out to the living room. "Good morning," Kennard said brightly. "Fancy seeing you all here."

Cronin laughed. "Nice of you to join us."

"Oh, leave him alone," Eiji said. "You and Alec are no better."

Cronin stared at him. "I had to put up with you and Jodis for a hundred years. You don't want to start."

Kennard looked at a pile of metal rods stacked up on his table, along with a fine dusting of rust. He made a face at it. "Is that a new sculpture? I hope you didn't pay too much for it."

Eiji held one up with a grin. "They are railroad spikes. Made of iron."

Stas took one in his hand, feeling its weight. "What are they for?"

Eiji held up two of them like daggers. "Weapons."

Alec laughed and Jodis sighed with a smile. "Do you want to know what we've found out about the sacred temple in India?"

Kennard nodded, and Stas wrapped his arm around Kennard's chest. "What we need weapons for? Will my Kennard be in danger? Like the creatures in the pits in Moscow?"

"No," Kennard replied. "Alec can see everything. He can even stop time. He's indestructible."

Stas nudged his nose to the back of Kennard's head. "Alec, yes. My Kennard, no."

"It'll be fine," Alec reassured them.

Kennard resisted sighing. "Care to share all the information, all-seeing-one, or are the rest of us just winging it?"

Alec grinned at him. "The Padmanabhaswamy temple is rather famous. Basically, it's a shrine to a Hindu god, and people have given their god offerings of gold and jewels for a very long time. Like a lot of gold and diamonds."

"Inside the temple?" Kennard asked. "Like vaults?"

"Yes. Many vaults. Some humans know about, some they don't."

"When was it built?" Stas asked.

"The first... vault, or crypt, if you like, is over two thousand years old," Alec answered. "It's been built over and fortified over the years. It holds the world's largest stash of treasure, ever."

"How much?" Kennard asked.

"The vaults they've managed to get opened had a combined value of over twenty-two billion."

Kennard's mouth fell open. "Dollars?"

Cronin snorted. "No, bitcoin."

Kennard stared at Cronin, then looked to Alec and sniffed. "I preferred him without the sense of humor. Is there a default setting we can reboot him to?"

Everyone laughed and Stas gave Kennard a squeeze. "Yes," Alec said. "I mean, no to the reboot, and yes to the twenty-two billion dollars. And that's US dollars."

Kennard was stunned. "Holy shit."

"They're convinced the vault they can't open has even more. They estimate a trillion dollars."

Kennard gave a low whistle. "How come we haven't heard of it before now?"

"Would you advertise that kind of wealth?" Cronin asked.

Kennard gave him a sidelong look. "I'm still a little raw from the bitcoin comment from you."

"I'm sure you'll get over it," Cronin said with a smirk. "Like that time you cost me ten half-merks and the innkeeper almost threw you out into the street. Into the sun. I paid your debt and you told me I'd get over it."

Kennard laughed. "That game of chance was rigged. The coin was weighted, and we both knew it. And anyway, you'd just robbed me of twice that over that silly Scottish skirmish."

"That silly Scottish skirmish was the Wars of the Three Kingdoms," Cronin said flatly. "Many Scots died."

"If the Scots lost," Eiji asked, "why did Cronin win the bet?"

"Because we bet on whose side the Irish would take," Cronin replied.

Kennard growled. "Fucking Irish."

Alec laughed. "Are you two done?"

Jodis sighed, long and loud. "They've been like this for five hundred years."

Stas chuckled again and Kennard leaned into him, giving Alec a nod. "Sorry, darling. Please go on. The Hindu temple with a few billion dollars in an unopened vault..."

"Not just unopened, but sealed shut," Alec said. "No locks or joins. They believe it can only be opened by the highest Hindu priests chanting the *Naga Bandham* mantra. Anyone else who tries to open it will be killed by snakes, but there are no high priests who can do it."

"Snakes?" Kennard asked, trying not to sound horrified.

"The Naga Bandham *is* a snake binding spell," Jodis added.

Kennard grimaced. "Oh good. Anyone fluent in *Parseltongue?*"

Alec laughed but no one else got the reference. He ignored the awkward silence and continued, "They guard the entrance, but lore has it that a few bandits tried to sneak in and, upon failing the mantra, snakes flooded the temple and attacked them."

"And we want to go there?" Kennard asked. He didn't care how horrified he sounded. "Because that doesn't sound too great to me. Quite frankly, anything that is sealed shut has been done so for good reason. Like the pyramids in Egypt and China."

"Well, yes," Alec went on. "But this isn't just sealed to protect the wealth."

"Why else be it sealed?" Stas asked.

"Oh," Kennard said flatly, realizing what Alec meant. "To keep someone in. A vampire vying for world domination, no doubt."

Alec grinned. "Yes. Indian folklore calls her a Yakshi, a blood drinking demon."

"So, a vampire," Kennard said. "Vying for world domination."

Alec shrugged but his smile said enough. "She guards the treasure. But the cobras coming to life is my first concern because, to date, that's never ended well."

Kennard was confused. "Wait. So the treasure of a trillion dollars is actually real?"

"Yep. They have an inventory from the 1600s or something."

"And there's a vampire who lives inside?" Stas asked.

Alec nodded. "Yep."

"And she's been trapped in there for how long?" Kennard asked. "How is she not dead? Or mad from starvation?"

"She has a gate."

Kennard blinked. "A gate? I thought you said it was sealed."

"It is. This gate is... more of a portal."

Kennard sagged with a loud sigh and he secured a wayward strand of hair. "Of course it is. Because when is it not weird with you."

Eiji laughed, and he handed an iron railroad spike to Jodis. "For you."

"Uh, what is rail spike for?" Stas asked.

Cronin answered, "Apparently this Yakshi has quite the aversion to iron."

"That's why the doors that are sealed shut and guarded by the cobras are made of iron," Jodis explained.

Then Alec added, "Though if you need to kill her, the iron spike must go through her head."

Kennard made a face. "Pretty sure that'd kill anyone, darling."

"I know, right?" Eiji's grin widened and he slid an iron spike into a thigh holster. "Let's go check it out!"

Kennard looked directly at Alec. *Is he okay? Eiji, I mean, mentally. Is he stable?*

Alec chuckled but coughed to cover it up. He gave Kennard a wink. *Come on. Let's go so he can have some fun.*

ALEC HAD SAID the temple would be dark and well-guarded, so before they appeared out of thin air on the security cameras, Alec did his stop-time trick, which Kennard had always found eerie.

The hall they appeared in had two guards armed with automatic rifles, but they were struck still, as if caught in a photograph. Jodis walked up to one and waved her hand in his face. He was utterly still. There were cameras as well, to which Eiji smiled at and made the peace sign. It made Kennard smile.

Stas must have been more shocked than he let on, because Alec looked right at him and clapped his arm. "Yes, I can stop time. It's taken some work and practice and it's draining, but I can do it."

Stas gave Kennard a look of wide-eyed wonder. "Your friends are weird." Stas shrugged. "Nice, but weird."

"I know, my love," Kennard replied. "You'll get used to them."

They all chuckled and Alec led them along a narrow hall to the door in question. It was huge and appeared to be made of iron. The cobras were in carved iron, intricate as the gargoyles had been, and framed the outside of the door, meeting at the top.

"They're not moving," Cronin said.

"They look like…" Eiji studied them, moving closer. "They look like *Watatsumi*. A Japanese dragon god."

"And like *Quetzalcoatl*," Jodis added quietly. "A serpent deity of the Mayan people."

"Hmmm," Alec hummed, his eyes closed. "Can you hear that?"

Kennard listened, as did everyone else. "Is that… water?"

"Sounds like the ocean," Cronin said.

"Yes." Jodis nodded. "I read on a website that Hindu lore says the sound is of the Atlantic. They said not everyone can hear it. Some hear the ocean tide; some hear the hissing of snakes."

"I'll take the tides of the ocean over snakes," Kennard said.

Alec put his hand to the door. "Shall we go inside?"

Eiji unsheathed two railroad spikes, one in each hand. "Yes. Let's go find ourselves a Yakshi."

Alec kept his hand on the door and bowed his head. Then he grimaced, like a twitch.

"Alec? What is it, m'cridhe?" Cronin asked, his concern evident on his face.

Alec frowned. "I can't leap in there." He gave Cronin a nod. "You try."

Cronin stood still for a second, then flinched. "I cannot."

"It's like a block or a void," Alec said with his hand to the door again. "I can see in there... I think. I'm not sure. But when I try to leap there, I keep getting an urge to go to a different place."

"Me too." Cronin frowned. "I've never encountered this before."

"Where does it tell you to go?" Jodis asked.

Alec answered, "To another temple, in Indonesia."

Cronin's gaze shot to Alec's. "Same. Bali, to be exact."

"Then let's go there," Eiji said impatiently. He tapped the iron cobra with the railroad spike, and with a screech of bending metal, the cobra raised its head, its hood spread wide, its fangs on display, and a hiss like grinding stone broke the silence. Everyone shot back a step, Stas keeping Kennard behind him, and Alec threw out his hand and the iron snake disintegrated into dust.

And in the next moment, time started again. Kennard turned to see if the guards had seen them, but before they had even turned around, Cronin reached out and grabbed him, and they were gone.

CHAPTER FOUR

THEY FOUND THEMSELVES OUTSIDE, the night sky above them filled with stars and around them green jungle and manicured lawn. Kennard knew Alec had stopped time again by the eerie stillness of the trees, but he glanced around and found a stone path leading up to an amazing stone entrance. "Where are we?"

"*Handara*," Alec replied, as though Kennard knew what that meant. "It's a golf club, of all the weird things."

"Bali," Cronin added.

"Thank you," Kennard said.

Eiji was facing the other way, squinting across the manicured golf course. "What's special about a golf course? If you want a game, I will win, just so you know."

Jodis nodded over his shoulder. "Look behind you."

The stone entrance itself was dark gray and worn by both weather and time. It consisted simply of two very tall, ornately carved pillars, wide at the base, narrow at the top. It looked like a gate or a doorway for giants. The backdrop was of mist-covered mountains, and it was beautiful.

"It's called a split gate," Alec explained.

When Stas took Kennard's hand, he looked up at him. "Are you okay, my love?"

Stas nodded, but he looked around warily. "Yes. Am fine. But I not like this."

"The leaping?" Kennard asked. "It takes some getting used to."

He nodded quickly. "I am used to knowing, hearing in minds what is happening. The silence is become weird."

"I can lift it," Alec said.

Stas gave him a nod, and then he blinked and glanced around a little bewildered. "Oh."

Kennard was certain Alec had lifted the shield. *Can you hear me, my love?*

Stas spun to look at him, took one step closer, grabbed his face in both hands, and kissed him.

Kennard broke the kiss with a laugh. "I take it that's a yes."

"My Kennard, I can hear you."

Kennard put his hand to his heart, then to his lips. *I love you.*

Stas laughed and wrapped him up in a crushing hug. "Oh, my Kennard." He mumbled into his neck, "*Slova ne mogut opisat' moyu lyubov k tebe.*"

Eiji squinted at them. "What did he say? I need to brush up on my Russian."

Alec answered, "He told Kennard no words could describe his love for him."

Eiji sighed. "Okay guys, we have work to do," he said. "Enough of the mushiness."

"Leave them alone," Jodis scolded him. "It's beautiful."

"Come on, this way," Alec said. "I can't hold time forever."

Stas put Kennard down and they all began to walk

along the path toward the temple, but then Stas reached over and pushed Eiji off balance. It might have been alarming—Jodis and Kennard both startled by their mates—but Eiji was laughing and Stas huffed but his lips twitched with a smile.

Alec chuckled, obviously having heard the whole silent exchange. "Any time you want me to block Eiji out, Stas. Just say the word."

"Not for now," Stas replied.

Are you okay, my love? Kennard asked.

Stas looked over to him and nodded with a smile, then he held out his hand for Kennard to hold. "I have long practice at blocking out nonsense."

Eiji laughed some more and went to the front of their group, leading the way as they went up the stone path. "It looks kinda creepy," Eiji said as he got to the pillars, dwarfed by their size, and before anyone could do or say anything, Eiji stepped through the gateway, turned around, and put his hands out. "But there's nothing weird about it," he said.

"The only weird thing in that doorway," Cronin said, "is you."

"Oh, ha ha," Eiji said. Jodis walked through and took Eiji's hand, pulling him along. Kennard looked ahead of Alec and Cronin at the split gate. It was ten meters high on each side, one meter wide, narrow at the top, and tapered down in step formation to a wider base. The stone was worn, eroded, hand-carved with gods and snakes, which was a little creepy but strangely ornate.

Cronin stepped through next, and he pointed to the carvings and turned to say something to Alec, but as soon as Alec stepped through the gate, he disappeared.

KENNARD AND STAS stopped on the last step, and Cronin swiped thin air. "Alec!"

Eiji's smile was gone, the two iron spikes now in his hands. Jodis was crouched in a battle stance, and Stas put his arm in front of Kennard. But Cronin...

He blinked in and out of view, as though he was leaping ten times a second, searching frantically. "Alec!" he screamed this time, as if his throat was raw, as if his heart was breaking.

But it was of no use. Alec was gone.

Jodis went to Cronin, and Kennard rushed for him too. Cronin was contorted in physical pain. "I can't feel him," Cronin gasped, his hand to his heart, then sucked back a harsh, deep breath.

"Wait," Stas said. "I hear something... In my mind. He calls for you."

They turned just as Alec stumbled out of thin air back out onto the path. He was wild-eyed and fearful until he saw Cronin. The relief between them was so palpable, Kennard could almost feel it. Alec turned and Cronin ran to him. Their embrace was so hard, so complete and heartfelt it brought tears to Kennard's eyes. Stas put his hand on Kennard's shoulder and Eiji put his arm around Jodis.

"I thought you gone, m'cridhe," Cronin whispered. "I couldn't feel you. Our bond was broken."

"I'm right here," Alec replied.

Jodis swallowed hard and her eyes shone with tears. "Let's never do that again."

"Agreed," Kennard said. He sagged into Stas' side and Stas was quick to hold him. A vampire's bond was a sacred, sacred thing. And to see it broken—even for just a moment

—to see the pain... it was something every mated vampire felt in their bones.

Cronin took Alec's face in his hands and kissed him, and it was then Kennard noticed time had restarted. Well, the trees were moving in the wind. But if it was moving when Alec had disappeared or if it started when he came back, Kennard couldn't be sure.

Eiji clapped Alec on the back. "Alec, my brother. Don't do that again."

Everyone took a moment to breathe, and Alec glanced up at Stas and nodded. "Yes, I'm fine. I just... they weren't kidding when they said that's a gateway."

"Where did you go?" Cronin asked. "What did you see?"

"I'll show you all," Alec said, then did that mind thing again when he showed visions, or in this case, memories, like a movie in everyone's mind. It was similar to this place, this temple, this jungle, but different. The lighting was different, like moonlight but brighter. It had a blueish-silver tint.

Then Kennard saw the moment Alec realized he was alone, that he couldn't see or feel Cronin, and a shattering blow of despair and loss followed like an ax to the chest. Kennard gasped at the pain and felt ill, and everyone reacted at the same time before Alec pulled the vision back. "Sorry," he said.

Stas growled and grabbed Kennard, pulling him in close, like he needed to physically hold him. Jodis gave a sharp cry, and Eiji looked as though he'd been shot. Afterwards, for a long moment, each couple stood in a silent embrace. "I never want to feel that again," Kennard said. "Jesus. Now I know what Jorge went through."

Everyone gave a solemn nod. Then Jodis said, "And

what I felt when Eiji decided to throw himself into sunlight to save Alec."

Eiji sighed. "I save Alec, I save the world, and I'm still in trouble," he joked, but his smile faded fast. He put his hand to Jodis' cheek. "My Jodis, I am sorry for causing you pain. I know now a fraction of what you went through."

She leaned into his touch, and Stas' arm tightened around Kennard. He turned in Stas' embrace and held him just as tight. *I will never leave you,* Kennard told him in his mind. *Not even for a second.*

"I won't do it again, either," Alec said, answering Kennard's private conversation. "I've been scared before, but nothing like that."

Then, still with one arm around Cronin, he reached out toward the gateway and slowly put his hand through.

His fingers disappeared first, then his knuckles, his thumb.

"What the fuck?" Kennard whispered.

Alec shot him a look of confusion. "I can see in your mind what you see. But it is not what I see." Then he looked at Eiji and Jodis. "What do you see?"

"Your hand is gone. It shimmers as though you're touching a wall of water," Jodis said. Eiji nodded.

Cronin frowned. "Disappears? How come I can still see it?"

Alec dropped his arm from around Cronin so no part of them touched, then Cronin gasped. "It's gone!" Then he touched Alec again, and he shook his head. "And it's back."

Kennard put his hand on Alec's arm, and instantly, he could see Alec's hand again. "God's hook!"

Cronin, Jodis, and Eiji all stopped, turned and stared disbelievingly at Kennard. "Did you just say God's hook?"

Cronin asked. He even almost smiled. "What century do you think this is?"

Kennard sighed. "It just slipped out."

"God's hook?" Eiji said with a laugh. "I haven't heard that for many, many years."

Kennard sniffed, his chin raised. "Go on, have your fun at my expense. I don't mind."

Eiji grinned at Kennard. "Verily, I a mere heathen understand. Ignore these huff-snuff cumber-worlds."

Cronin smiled at that, and Jodis chuckled and put her hand on Kennard's arm. "You have to admit, Eiji mastering English in medieval times was kind of funny."

Kennard sighed dramatically, but the smile he was fighting won out. "It was, and still is, a sacrilege to the King's English."

Cronin shrugged. "It would have been. Except at the time, the King of England was Scottish."

Kennard sighed the mother of all sighs, but Stas chuckled. Kennard gave him a questioning look. "Is funny," Stas said.

"Ah, guys," Alec said. He now had his whole arm through the gateway, then one leg. "Stas, take Cronin's arm and don't let go."

Stas grabbed Cronin just as Alec pulled him through, and this time when Alec disappeared through the gateway, Cronin did too, all but the arm that Stas still had hold of. Then they came back out. "It's what I thought," Alec explained. "Whoever is touching me can come through as well."

"I could see in there," Stas said.

Alec nodded. "Because you were touching Cronin. If we all form a link, we can all come through."

"We could," Jodis said. "But should we? I mean, what if we can't get back?"

"Stay here," Alec said, grabbed Cronin's hand, and pulled him through the gateway. They literally disappeared into the thin air, and then a moment later, they came back through. "It works the same," Alec said. "If we're touching, we'll be fine." Then he made a face. "I think."

"You think?" Kennard asked.

"Since when do you not know?" Jodis asked. "You know everything; you can see everything."

"Not in there I can't." He looked at each of them, then shrugged. "I have no powers in there."

Cronin shook his head. "I don't like it."

"I can hear you in there," Stas said. "In my mind. I hear your mind when you are in there. It's small, like distant noise, but now that I know what it is, I know it's you."

"That's good to know," Alec said; then he got that far-off look in his eyes, as though he was seeing things no one else could. "The guards at the Indian temple have discovered the cobra. They're going to force open the doors. If we're going to stop the Yakshi from escaping, we need to move now."

"How?" Cronin said. "By going through these gateways? Into some different dimension?"

Alec nodded. "I think so. When I try to see into the locked vault. It takes me here, to this gateway."

"And if we don't stop them?" Kennard asked. "If we let the humans open it? What happens?"

"The Yakshi will kill any human who tries to enter," he replied. "And who knows where she'll stop?"

Kennard sighed again. "Vampire domination and the mass murder of humans who attempt to steal gold that is not theirs. I don't have a problem with that," he said. Eiji laughed and Stas chuckled, but Kennard knew allowing this woman to wreak havoc in the public eye was against vampire law. "But whatever."

"So, are we doing this?" Alec asked. Everyone nodded. He took Cronin's hand and gave a nod. "Hold on."

Each holding the hand of the person in front of them, forming a chain, they walked through the gateway and into what Kennard was certain was a different place. It was still blueish but now they stood in a temple. Stone walls, carvings of gods and more snakes. "Where are we?" he asked.

"*Pura Besakih* temple," Alec answered. "Still in Bali, Indonesia."

"But not near the first gates?" Jodis asked.

Alec shook his head. "No. Miles apart."

"So the gateways are teleporting gates? Like a wormhole in space?" she pressed.

"But only for Alec," Cronin said. "We can't enter without him. He's the... key."

"I'm really beginning to hate that word," Alec mumbled.

Kennard took in his surroundings. This temple had many levels, at many different heights. There were lush gardens, manicured lawns, many ponds of water and pools, and many more stone walls and statues. Though in the distance, at the far end of the temple was another split-gateway. "I'm guessing we're supposed to go through that one?"

Alec gave a nod. "I think so."

A breeze caught them, rustling the palms; time was not stopped. The air was warm and humid, but there was no scent of humans. Stas must have read Kennard's mind because he said, "No humans here."

Eiji held his iron spikes in his hands, fisting them like

daggers, and Jodis carried one as well. Kennard and Stas both took theirs to hand as well.

"Wait," Cronin said. They all stopped still. "I want to try something." Then squinted in concentration, then shook his head. "I cannot leap here."

"I cannot hear minds," Stas said with a shake of his head.

Jodis flicked her hand out toward the fish pond. "My talent is gone also."

"Well, no one needs me to read their DNA, so...," Eiji said.

"Oh, so now you all know what it's like to have no powers," Kennard whined. "I'm just dull and boring and powerless no matter which dimension we're in."

Cronin snorted. "You are far from dull and boring, Kennard."

"You have power over me," Stas said with a shy smile. "If any consolation."

Kennard gave him a wink. "Thank you, my love."

"I have no powers here," Alec said. "None." Then he shuddered. "It's very disconcerting. I feel like I'm naked or exposed. I thought my talents were a burden, but I feel very unprotected without them."

"It's only temporary," Cronin said. "And if we need to, we hightail it back to that gate."

Alec nodded slowly. "But don't you think it's weird? I mean, what's blocking me in here?"

"You've met you, right?" Kennard said to Alec. "If something is going to be weird, darling, it's going to be you. Or happen to you. Or just you in general."

Eiji laughed and Alec shot him a pointed stare. "What?" Eiji said. "It's true."

Water splashed in the pond beside them and they all

spun toward the sound, just in time for Kennard to see a tail of some kind slither into the pool. "Did you see that?" he whispered.

"Yes," everyone answered.

Eiji ran to the edge of the pond, crouching low and holding his iron spikes in each hand. "I see it," he said and slowly moved along the pool edge.

Then a snake burst up from the water toward him, but before Eiji could react, Jodis threw out her hand and tried to freeze the pond, but her powers didn't work. The snake thrashed violently upward, a growling hissing sound escaped it, and Eiji struck it with an iron spike. The snake shattered into rubble and into the water. Eiji re-holstered his iron spike and snatched up a handful of rubble out of the water. He held it out for us all to see. "Stone."

"Like the gargoyles," Jodis said.

"And the Terracotta Army," Cronin added.

"It was a snake but not a snake," Stas said. "Like dragon."

Alec looked up at Stas and nodded. "Yes. Or like the stone carvings from Hindu and Mayan history."

Kennard nodded. "I don't think I'm going to like how this ends."

Cronin scanned their surroundings. "Me either," he said. "I think we should keep moving."

Alec nodded and started toward the end of the temple, toward the other split gate. "This way."

They raced up some stone steps to the highest platform of the open temple. A wall ran along their right, a pond to their left. A stone snake slithered out of the pond, through the split gate ahead of them.

"Holy shit," Kennard said, as they all slowed to a stop. "Tell me you all saw that."

Alec, Cronin, and Eiji nodded. "We saw," Jodis replied.

"Do we follow?" Stas asked.

Alec gave a nod. "I am drawn to the gate, like part of me knows we have to keep going. I don't know why or what's beyond the next gate. I can't see past it."

"Then let's get this over with," Cronin said. "The renovations on our house in Scotland were recently finished, and I can't wait to get back there."

"I've been meaning to ask," Kennard said. "But Stas and I were..."

"Busy?" Alec said.

"I was going to say indisposed," Kennard said flatly.

Eiji pretended to be shocked, gasped and put his hand to his heart. "God's hook!"

Kennard sighed and looked up at Stas. "You know how I said these were my friends and I missed them?"

Stas nodded. "Yes."

"Well, not nearly as much as I remembered."

Cronin laughed and clapped Kennard on the back. "We missed you too." Then he nodded pointedly at Eiji. "If you want to get back at Eiji, ask him how fast he drove that sports car."

Eiji looked equally shocked and offended. "I drove fast. Like lightning."

"Sure," Alec agreed. "If lightning struck at one mile per hour."

Jodis sighed loudly, her shoulders sagged. "Must we do this now?" She took out her iron spike and began walking to the gate. "I'm going to see if there's anything I can stab."

Eiji followed after her. "Jodis, wait! I drove fast, didn't I? You tell them!" he cried as they reached the next split gate.

Cronin laughed and gave Kennard a nudge. "He was so bad. You should have seen him."

Kennard chuckled. "Stas has an old truck, maybe Eiji might like to drive it."

"I hope you like first gear," Alec murmured.

Eiji turned to face them with his arms folded. "I can hear you!"

Alec laughed and held out his hand for everyone to link up, and together they all slipped through the gate. Immediately to their left, another stone snake slithered into the pond. There were lily pads and lotuses, and ordinarily, Kennard would have thought it a scenic place, but now it seemed alive. And not in a good way.

Eiji and Jodis went to the pond, and after inspecting it, Jodis turned and shook her head. "It's gone."

But as she turned her back to the pond, a stone snake burst out of the water, aiming directly for Jodis. Eiji flew through the air, iron spikes in both hands, and struck the creature before it reached Jodis. He landed neatly in a fight-ready stance and Jodis spun around, spike in hand. She gave Eiji a nod and stood at ease, then stepped in close to him, put her hand to his face, and whispered something Kennard couldn't hear.

He gave her a smile, then looked over at Alec and Cronin. "You think I'm slow," Eiji said. "Nice of you all to show up." He slipped a spike into his thigh holster and put his hand up in a stop motion. "No, no, don't bother. I took care of it. Because you were slow, and I was fast."

"Are you okay, Jodis?" Cronin asked.

"Yes, thanks to Eiji," she answered quietly. "It was a little closer than I'd have liked."

"Another snake," Kennard said. "Or serpent. Or dragon.

I don't know what they are. When it came out of the water and saw us, it wasn't happy we were here."

"Where are we now?" Stas asked, looking around.

"Tikal, Guatemala," Alec answered, staring up at the tall pyramid ruins before them.

"Oh, good. Another pyramid," Kennard mumbled. Though he was glad they were in this weird time-slip dimension because the blueish-silver hue meant it wasn't direct sunlight, considering they'd stumbled out and were now standing out in the open.

Alec gave a nod. "And uh, this is the temple of the two-headed snake."

"Of course it is." Kennard nodded, wondering why no one else thought this was crazy.

"So weird," Stas mumbled. Cronin nodded, as did Jodis, but Eiji seemed to be in his element.

Kennard took in his surroundings. They were standing in front of a tall, thin stone pyramid in the middle of a jungle. Narrow stairs ran up the center to a dark doorway at the very top.

Heavily eroded, much of the carvings had been washed away, though it was easy to see what they had once been. The long serpent body was still discernible.

"At least there's no water here," Cronin said. "No pools or moats."

"The Mayans surrounded their temples with reservoirs," Jodis answered.

And sure enough, right on bloody cue, rustling sounds came out of the jungle. Snakes slithered up out of the water toward them, moving faster than their stone bodies should have allowed. They skimmed across the ground, back and forth, slithering and hissing, fangs bared, with angry eyes.

Jodis slid along the ground toward the first one and

stabbed a spike into its body, just below its head, while Stas stood in front of Kennard and smashed an iron spike into the side of the second snake's head.

But the sound of snapping and grinding stone echoed around them and more creatures came at them. "Come on!" Alec cried. "Through the door."

As they ran up the stairs on the pyramid to the next doorway, another stone serpent slipped through ahead of them. Alec stopped right at the door at the top. Kennard didn't dare look back at the snakes that were now ascending the stairs. "I don't know what's on the other side," Alec said. He held out his hand, and they all touched hands and went through the door.

CHAPTER FIVE

THE TEMPLE WAS OLDER and more ruin than building, and the jungle was different. The air and humidity, the angle of the moon were all different. It was still dark, thankfully, but this time Kennard knew where they were. He'd seen pictures of this place before, but he could hardly believe his eyes. "Is this Angkor Wat? Are we in—"

"Cambodia," Alec whispered.

They all stood there and took in their surroundings. The historic Cambodian temple was incredible. The largest stone temple on the planet; a true testament to the engineering and craftsmanship of the Khmer Empire. There were stone walls, ornate temples, statues of Buddha, gods, and huge stone faces in walls. There were stone paths, open doorways, small temples, larger ones, statues of humans, elephants, immense wall carvings, and a lot of statues of snakes.

Which Kennard hadn't considered as odd. Until now.

The land around them was flat and densely forested, and the temple itself was huge. "There are no ponds in the temples here," Jodis noted.

"Not exactly. The entire temple is surrounded by water," Alec said. "A huge moat."

And right on cue, a large stone snake slithered out of the jungle and up the steps toward them. Kennard could see it better now, given he had a few moments to look at it as it approached. It was a serpent, that was certain. But it wasn't a normal snake. It looked almost like a legless dragon. Not like a gargoyle so much, but more like the creatures that were littered throughout Asian histories. And South American histories and Egyptian... Its huge fangs were bared, its eyes angry, and it reared up as it approached, moving faster than its stone form should have allowed. It was also wet.

"It came from the moat," Eiji said, holding the iron spikes in both hands. "Be careful, my love. It is much bigger than the others," he said to Jodis.

They separated, splitting their target mass to attack the creature from both sides. Stas moved closer to Kennard in a defensive way, and he and Kennard stood almost back to back, prepared to defend each other. Alec and Cronin did the same. The stone creature hissed and growled a stone-grating sound, but it was no match for Jodis and Eiji. They were too skilled, too in sync, and they both flew through the air in a graceful, violent ballet, stabbing the snake and crumbling it to dust.

But then another slithered toward them, and another. Kennard could see them rear up out of the water, searching for them. Then as the creatures faced them, they made their way out of the moat, coming straight for them. The way they moved with their heads raised reminded Kennard of something.

"Cronin, darling," Kennard said flatly. "Is there anything about the Loch Ness monster you'd like to share with us?"

Alec snorted but Cronin frowned. "Assumed folklore," he replied. "But there is a resemblance."

Kennard didn't even try to hide his surprise. "Have you seen the Loch Ness monster? Why have you never mentioned it?"

Cronin rolled his eyes. "Resemblance to supposed pictures, Kennard. Do you not think it would have come up in conversation or a wager before now?"

"Ah, guys?" Eiji said. "I hate to interrupt your pointless bickering, but do you think you might lend us a hand?"

Kennard chuckled. "You and Jodis seem to have everything under control."

Another creature slithered from their right this time, not from directly ahead, and Stas leaped to it and smashed it with his iron nail spike. "Stas has under control," Stas said.

Kennard took a moment to appreciate his lover's form. His huge frame, his grace, his focus. "And what a mighty fine sight that is."

Cronin groaned. "Please spare us."

"Spare you?" Kennard quipped back. "I seem to recall you two"—he waved his iron spike between Cronin and Alec—"getting a certain kind of handsy with little regard to who saw. Remember that time in the alley behind my nightclub."

Alec smashed a stone snake and shot Kennard a look. "Really? We're going to talk about this now? Perhaps you could lend a hand here. I mean, I'd hate for you to get your nails dirty."

Kennard inspected his fingernails. "Thank you for thinking of me, and you're doing such a fabulous job." But just then, out of the corner of his eye, he saw a stone serpent slither out of the grass, almost at Stas. Kennard sprang toward it, slid the final meters on the ground on his knees, then struck the beast with his spike, obliterating it to dust. When he stood, his leg had mud and dirt from his Italian boot to his knee.

Alec stared at him before he broke out in a grin. "I've got you figured out, Kennard. You feign diffidence and apathy, but I know better. You're all heart."

Stas killed another beast. "I could tell you that. My Kennard is biggest heart." Then Stas turned to Kennard. "Thank you for killing snake near me."

Kennard wiped Stas' cheek, swiping away some dirt. "Anything for you, my love."

"Okay, we need to leave," Jodis said. "They're not stopping. Wherever they came from, whatever made them decide to become active now, is not stopping."

"I don't see another split gate," Cronin said, looking all around. "Where do we go?"

"This way," Alec said, running toward the front of the temple where a land bridge crossed the moat. "I don't know why."

"Shouldn't we be running away from the stone snakes?" Eiji asked as they all ran. "Not toward them?!"

Kennard liked Eiji's question but they all followed Alec and Cronin. "Be careful," Cronin called out, striking a serpent as it flew up and out of the water toward Alec. Kennard took out one, as did Stas. Jodis and Eiji scored two each. They soon cleared the moat and Alec led them into the deep, thick jungle. It wasn't the smell of the jungle, damp and rotting undergrowth, or the sounds of the jungle in particular that Kennard noticed. "What is that foul stench? And that unholy racket."

"Monkeys," Alec said.

They stopped running, and Jodis looked up at Alec. "Why are they not frozen in time?"

"I don't know," Alec whispered. "I don't know why any of this makes zero sense. But it looks as though the snakes haven't followed us."

"Or they can't," Jodis added.

"Or they're surrounding us," Kennard added. Everyone shot him a look and he shrugged. "Let's not pretend any of this is remotely normal. I'm not ruling out anything."

"Which way do we go now, m'cridhe?" Cronin asked. "The sooner we figure out what exactly is at play here, the sooner it will be over."

Alec put his hand to his forehead and scanned the jungle, but before he could reply, a screech of monkeys erupted to their right, deeper in the jungle. "Monkeys not happy. I say we follow noise," Stas said.

"Good idea," Alec replied.

They ran farther into the jungle and came to what looked like a long-forgotten temple. There were stone walls in disrepair, perhaps a thousand years old. Tree roots covered stone blocks as though the temple was being swallowed by the forest. Broken Buddha and Vishnu statues held hostage by trees and undergrowth, stone walls were overcome and broken; centuries of neglect and weather had done no favors to what Kennard thought could have once been a beautiful temple. Now its beauty was a testament to its age. A different kind of beauty, a loveliness in its demise. Not unlike himself, Kennard allowed. He'd been old and worn by the world, wallowing in loneliness, swallowed up and strangled by his own possessions until Stas came into his life.

Stas came to an abrupt stop, making everyone else stop as well. "Kennard?" he said, cradling Kennard's face. "Why you feel sad?"

Kennard had forgotten that Stas was attuned to his

emotions. "Not sadness," Kennard replied. He kissed Stas' palm. "More of an acknowledgment of the history here, how it's been forgotten, erased. How the same can come of us if we allow it. I didn't mean to cause you any concern."

Stas gave a nod. "You are okay?"

Kennard smiled up at him. "Yes, my love."

"It is eerie how the jungle is reclaiming the land as its own," Jodis conceded.

"It looks like the set of Jumanji," Alec added. "Or Lara Croft."

"What is those things? Jumanji and Lara Croft?" Stas asked with a frown.

Kennard chuckled as they began to walk again, following the raucous sound of screeching monkeys. "Don't worry, my love. Alec is prone to bursts of popular culture references. A product of his time." Then Kennard shot Alec a pointed glare. "And how is it that Alec can say such things and no one makes an issue of it, and I say 'God's hook' once in four hundred years and everyone points it out?"

Eiji laughed. "Don't worry, we mock him too."

"You're the oldest of all of us, Eiji," Kennard said, stepping over a huge tree root. "How is it you even understand his popular culture references?"

"A lot of times I just smile and nod. I have no clue what he means. But some things I know. Like Lara Croft because we play on Xbox."

"Shhh," Cronin whispered. Everyone stopped walking, stopped talking, and listened.

The monkeys were quiet.

The entire jungle was silent.

"Hurry," Alec said as he took off, faster, treading without a sound, like the stealthy hunters that vampires were. Kennard was well aware they were following Alec even though he was going into this blind. And they would follow him regardless, as Kennard knew they always would. As he knew *he* always would. Alec stopped in a small clearing, fronted by an ancient stone wall with three doorways. Three rectangles, the middle one slightly larger, laced with tree roots, were all but part of the jungle. Three mystic doorways built many hundreds of years ago, doorways that seemed to only lead to inky blackness.

"Oh, let me guess," Kennard deadpanned. "We're going through them, aren't we?"

Alec gave a hard nod. He seemed to be a little out of breath, more concerned than Kennard could recall seeing him, certainly not since his human days. And Kennard realized that being without his powers must have been frightening for Alec. He was leading them, his mate and best friends, into the unknown, into a realm in which he had no powers, no advantage. Kennard had never had powers to lose, but he could appreciate that it must be hard and he regretted his joking and nonchalance. He gave Alec a serious look. "If you say we go through them, then that's what we do. As weird as this whole dimension thing is, and as much as I might doubt our collective sanity, I have never doubted you, Alec. Not even when you were human."

Alec gave him an acknowledging smile and Cronin put his hand on Alec's shoulder but mouthed *thank you* to Kennard.

Kennard gave him a wink, then taking Stas' hand, they followed Alec and Cronin through the center doorway just as a huge black panther leaped to sit atop the stone slab above the doorways. Stas balked at it, and even Kennard had to admit he was not expecting to see a huge cat sitting there now licking its paw as though he'd been expecting them.

Alec walked up to it. "Hey there, pretty kitty," he said.

The jaguar began to purr. He swished his tail down over the edge of the platform above the doors and yawned, showing every tooth. Alec chuckled. "Are you guarding these doorways for us?"

"It would explain the disrupted monkeys," Cronin said, walking up to stand beside Alec. "Who are now markedly absent and silent."

"These three doorways," Jodis said. "They are the same as in Mexico."

"The pyramids?" Kennard asked.

Jodis nodded. "And Peru."

"And Egypt," Alec added. "And Jordan. The city of Petra also has doors like this."

"I don't like it," Eiji said.

"Neither do I," Cronin added.

The jaguar purred louder and Alec turned to the others. "We need to go through them," Alec said. "This is where we need to go."

"For who?" Stas asked. "Who has led us here?"

Kennard nodded. "Yes. Alec, you say you don't know why, but something is telling you where to go. Shouldn't we question who?"

"This Yakshi woman?" Cronin said with a shrug. "I assume. This started with the golden temple in India. The temple she supposedly guards. Would it not stand to reason that she'd be behind this?"

"Perhaps," Kennard allowed. "Disregarding the split gates that can teleport us to different countries, because that's a whole conversation for another time, maybe we should be asking broader questions such as why are your talents absent here? What is this dimension or time-slip? And what is the Yakshi's purpose for drawing us here? If it is even her. Every other megalomaniac vampire who wanted to kill Alec before was simply the puppet of an even bigger megalomaniac vampire who was vying for the usual world domination or to transfer his powers."

"You think someone's using her?" Alec asked.

Kennard gave a shrug. "It would hardly be surprising."

Then the jaguar began to growl. It stood to attention and stared off into the jungle, baring its teeth and growling. The rustle of leaves and screeching of monkeys started again. "Something's coming," Alec said. "We should go."

The jaguar leaped down and padded between them, facing the jungle at whatever threat was coming. It hissed and raised its front paw, claws at the ready, just as the first creature came through the jungle.

Snakes. A lot of them. The sound of grinding stone as they slithered was almost as loud as the raspy hissing. "Shit," Eiji said. "I mean, God's hook!"

Cronin snorted and Kennard sighed. "Will I ever live that down?"

Stas pulled Kennard closer, but Alec was already at the middle doorway. "We need to leave, now!" He grabbed Cronin's hand, who grabbed Jodis, who grabbed Eiji, then Stas and Kennard, and their chain disappeared through the doorway and into something Kennard had never seen before, not as human or vampire, in all his years.

It was black, dark even for his vampire sight, and eerily silent.

"Well, this is creepy," Eiji said.

"Stay close," Alec whispered from the front. "There's something up ahead."

Kennard drew on his senses. His sight was diminished in the darkness but his hearing and olfactory senses were just fine. There was a dripping sound far-off, echoing in what must have been a vast space. An empty space. The smell of dust and old death filled his nose as they walked out of the darkened corridor into a cavernous room.

There was no light, but Kennard's vampire vision allowed him to see where they were. He turned back to the corridor they'd walked out of to see nothing but a split gate, like those in Indonesia, painted on the wall. "What the hell?"

Alec went back to the wall and, reaching out slowly, put his hand through the stone. "It's a gateway."

"But it's painted on," Eiji said.

"I didn't say it made sense," Alec replied.

The air was dank and hot. The floor, walls, and roof were stone, and Cronin walked to the far corner where something—a blanket or cloak—lay crumpled on the ground. "Be careful," Alec whispered.

Cronin slowly lifted the fabric and frowned. "Dust. Vampire dust."

"Someone died here?" Jodis asked.

Cronin held up an iron arrow. "Someone was killed here." He stood up and surveyed the walls. "And look at this," he said, holding up a gold circular armband or neck collar. He held it out to Jodis and she took it with a frown.

"It's Egyptian, and it's old. These hieroglyphs are at least two thousand years old."

"Are we in Egypt?" Kennard asked.

Alec shook his head. "No."

Kennard nodded pointedly to the Egyptian jewelry. "Then how is that possible?"

"I don't know," Alec replied.

Eiji scanned the room. "There is no way in or out. How did they get in here?"

"Yes, there is," Alec said, nodding toward the far wall.

Another split gate was painted on the wall. "It looks different. Shimmering almost. Can you not see that?"

Kennard stared at the wall. He could see the painting, but there was no shimmering. Just dull ochre paintings. "No," he replied.

Everyone shook their heads. "It doesn't shimmer, m'cridhe," Cronin said.

"It does for me," Alec whispered.

"It must be visible only to the key," Jodis said.

There were other paintings on the wall that Kennard was certain he'd seen before. Dragons and serpents, a mix of those he'd seen in Indonesia and Japan, like the stone snakes they'd run away from in Cambodia, were painted on the walls. Red and yellow and green, faded but clear enough to give Kennard the creeps. And above the snakes, inscribed almost like hieroglyphics, was writing he was not familiar with. "It looks like ancient temple art. Hindu or Mayan," he mused. "But that writing... I don't know what that is."

"Me either," Jodis whispered. A cold trickle of fear ran down Kennard's spine. If Jodis didn't know what it was...

Stas looked around the huge room, keeping Kennard close at all times. "Where in the hell is this?"

Alec walked into the center of the room and looked up. On the ceiling was a painted circle. Large in size, intricate in detail, was a painted version of the Sun Stone. "I know where we are," he said. Then he turned and smiled at them. "We're in Mexico."

"Mexico?" Eiji repeated.

Alec nodded. "Teotihuacan, Central Mexico." He pointed up to the painting. "It's similar to the Chinese one we found under Qi's pyramid. Only it's Aztec."

"The pyramids of Mexico," Jodis murmured.

Alec gave her a nod. "We're directly under the Pyramid of the Sun."

"How you know this?" Stas asked.

Alec shrugged. "I don't know. I have no powers here, but I know where we are as I know my own name. I can't explain it."

"But we were just in Cambodia," Kennard said. "On the other side of that painted doorway."

"It's fascinating," Jodis said. "And suddenly it makes sense why some Asian, Mayan and Incan, and Egyptian gods and statues, religions, and cultures are all so similar, yet thousands of miles apart."

Cronin made a thoughtful face. "And perhaps why or how they all disappeared."

Everyone stood in silence, giving that idea the thought it deserved. "At least nothing is trying to kill us in here," Kennard said.

And then, right on cue, the painted snakes on the walls began to move.

CHAPTER SIX

"RUN!" Alec said as the painted snakes all slithered down the walls to the floor and formed a macabre moving painted carpet, slithering toward them. They each grabbed hands once more and Alec ran straight at the painted door on the wall and, because things weren't weird enough, they passed right through solid stone into a long, darkened tunnel. Kennard was the last through, and he turned around to see if any snakes had followed. Thankfully none had.

"Are we all good?" Alec asked. Everyone nodded. "Good, good," Alec mumbled. "And I swear, if we come out at Platform 9¾, I'll be paying J.K. Rowling a visit."

Kennard was the only one who chuckled; no one else seemed to get the joke. "Right," Kennard said. "If he's still making Harry Potter references in four hundred years and no one takes the piss, I'll be bitterly disappointed in all of you."

"Oh, Harry Potter!" Eiji said. "Now I get it." He looked at Kennard. "Harry Potter references are allowed. Saying 'God's hook', not so much."

"Eiji," Kennard droned. "Remember that time when I said I was thankful for having you as a friend?"

Eiji nodded, grinning.

"I take it back."

Eiji's smile faded into a frown, and Jodis sighed. "Are you two done? I swear, somedays it's like being a preschool teacher." Eiji and Kennard both smirked.

"Where are we now?" Cronin asked.

"There are tunnels that run from the Pyramid of the Sun to the Pyramid of the Moon," Alec said.

"These tunnels were only recently discovered," Jodis explained. "But they were inaccessible because of huge boulders that had been put in place to block the doorways."

"Huge boulders with painted doorways that Alec can apparently walk through," Eiji added.

"Come on," Alec said. "Let's keep moving."

The tunnel itself was only wide enough for single file, and poor Stas had to duck his head. "Are you okay, my love?" Kennard asked him.

"No snakes, so is good," he replied. "Though I not like tunnels much. Like pits under Moscow church. Not much good comes from dark places."

"The second one is just up ahead," Alec said. "There's another boulder blocking the way. We'll need to walk through it, so hold hands."

They formed a chain and, again, simply followed Alec through the stone wall into another large underground chamber. It was slightly smaller than the first one, and it too was constructed of stone.

"This is the Pyramid of the Moon," Alec said. "Well, under it. About thirty feet."

Instead of having snakes painted on the walls, this one had carved stone snakes instead. "Ah, Alec...?" Eiji said, staring at the walls, his pitch higher. "There are snakes. Like the cobras on the temple door in India. But stone."

"I see them," he said.

"And look," Cronin said, nodding toward another pile of dust nearby. He nudged it with his foot and unearthed a wooden spike. He picked it up, inspected it, his expression one of horror. "It's hawthorn."

"The Illyrians?" Jodis hissed. "What the hell went on here?"

"*When* the hell did this go on?" Kennard added.

"I don't know," Alec said. "And I'm not sure I want to find out."

Eiji was still staring at the stone serpents that lined the walls. "Can we get out of here before they move?"

Then ever so slowly the carvings began to creak and dust fell to the floor as stone ground against stone. "Too late!" Kennard cried.

"Move, move!" Jodis yelled as they ran for the far wall.

It looked like nothing but a solid stone wall to Kennard. And to Cronin, apparently. "Alec," he cried, his tone full of warning.

"I can see it," he replied as he slipped through the stone wall as though it was nothing but a hologram.

They found themselves in another tunnel, similar to the last. All of them wide-eyed and wary. "This is getting a little too weird," Cronin said. "Even for us."

"Agreed," Alec said. "This tunnel leads us to where we need to go. I can feel it."

"What do you mean *feel it*, m'cridhe?" Cronin asked.

"I'm not sure," he answered. "But I'm drawn to this. As though my blood is drawn to it."

And when they walked through the long tunnel and out into the underground chamber, Kennard could see why.

Everyone stood there silent, taking in the room before them. A foreign yet strangely familiar sight.

"Holy shit," Kennard said.

"How is this possible?" Jodis asked.

"What is it?" Stas asked.

"This is exactly what lies beneath the Chinese pyramid, only the Chinese one mimics the Chinese landscape. It was where Khan and his Terracotta Army were," Kennard replied.

In this chamber, the huge space was made of earth: clay walls and dirt floors which mimicked the topography above them on a miniature scale. Hills, mountains, pyramids.

And rivers of mercury.

"Alec, what is this place?" Eiji asked.

"We're under the third pyramid at Teotihuacan," he whispered. "It's called the Temple of the Feathered Serpent."

"Feathered serpent," Kennard repeated. "As in snakes with feathers. As in snakes that can *fly*? Because I don't want to be around for that, thank you very much."

Stas pulled Kennard against him and Kennard went willingly. He felt a thousand times better just touching Stas but having his huge arm around him so protectively was everything he needed right then. "Where is that writing from?" Stas asked, pointedly nodding up to what resembled cave art, scrawled in brown-red ochre paint. No, wait...

"Is that blood?" Alec asked.

"Possibly," Cronin said. "It's too old to tell. The scent is long-faded."

"What does it say?" Eiji asked, turning to Jodis.

She shook her head. "I don't know. It looks a mix of Ancient Greek and Mayan. It's nothing I've ever seen before."

Cronin went to the corner where several clumps of dust lay in time-forgotten mounds. He picked up a necklace of turquoise, amber, and feathers. He thumbed an inscription on one of the beads. "This looks Aztec."

Alec went to another mound of dust and collected what looked like a few coins. He blew the dust away and his eyes went wide. "What are these?"

He handed them to Jodis and her mouth fell open. "Uninscribed coins. Lydian, if I recall." She looked up at the faces watching her. "Anatolian, which is now Turkey. Perhaps 600BC."

"Holy shit," Kennard said again.

"God's hook," Eiji said.

Kennard rolled his eyes but ignored him. "What does that mean?"

"I would assume from the mounds of dust, or murdered vampires, that these split gates and dimension doorways have been used for thousands of years." Alec looked around the chamber. "By people or vampires from all over the world."

"To travel far and stay out of sunlight," Stas added.

Alec nodded. "I think so."

"But wouldn't they need to be a key?" Jodis asked. "Only you can get through these gateways. We're only here because of you."

Alec frowned. "Unless it's a power or talent that I never knew I had." He shrugged. "I can't use any powers in here, so I'm as clueless about this as you guys."

"At least there are no snakes here," Eiji said.

A bubbling noise popped behind them, and they all spun to the sound to see one of the mercury pools take form. It bubbled again, and then a mercury snake rose up out of the pool. It was misshapen at first, but after a second it formed and showed its fangs and hissed a wet, liquid sound.

"You had to say it, didn't you?" Kennard growled. He moved out of Stas' arms and stood defensively in front of him.

And then another pool of mercury began to bubble, and another, and another liquid silver snake rose from the ground.

"Where the hell is the gate out of here?" Jodis asked.

Kennard scanned the walls, but he could see no split gate or triple doorway. "There isn't one."

"Wait," Alec said, holding his hands up. "Look at them."

The snakes weren't coming for them. They were slithering away to the far side and sinking into the hard earth-pressed wall.

"The split gate," Alec whispered. "Can you see it?"

Everyone shook their heads. "No," Cronin replied. "Alec, we cannot."

Then a snake did the strangest thing. It stopped, looked back toward Alec as though it was waiting for him, then disappeared into the wall. "They want me to go with them," Alec said. "This way."

"Stop, Alec," Cronin murmured. "Do you think it wise to follow them?"

"It's pulling me toward them. The mercury in my blood...," he said. He gave a hard nod and smiled. "I'm certain of it. This is where all these gates lead to. This is the last one."

Alec started for the split gate only he could see, and everyone followed. They jumped over rivers of mercury, careful not to step on any quicksilver snakes. They all took the hand in front of them, and Alec led them through the wall of earth, and when they appeared on the other side, Kennard stopped and stared.

Gold. So much of it, it was hard to see where one item stopped and the next started. Gold walls, gold tables, chairs, piles of coins, goblets, jewelry, trinkets, everything was gold. There was a gold statue of a man lying down on a bed of cobras, and the serpents rose up over his head. It must have weighed several tons. But that wasn't the most amazing thing.

A woman stood in the center of it all. She was beautiful, even more beautiful than Jodis. She shimmered gold; her white flowing sari was gold; her dark hair was somehow gold, fluid and moving. The mercury snakes slid toward her, melding into her feet, becoming part of her. Kennard realized then that the snakes hadn't been chasing them in all the different jungles and temples, they were coming here. They were coming to her.

Snakes of stone and snakes of gold slithered through the jewels and coins, wrapping themselves around table legs and golden trunks of treasure. It was horrifying yet the woman was completely at ease with them. She smiled and held out her hands in welcome, and it was then that Kennard noticed the irises of her eyes. They were vertical slits, as if the snakes that melded into her body had become a part of her.

"The key," she said, her voice musical. "I've been waiting for you."

Alec gave a nod as though he was meeting royalty. "It has been quite the journey to reach you," he said. "Please call me Alec. You are the Yakshi?"

She bowed her head. "I am. My name is Manasa," she said. When she lifted her head, her smile showed her fangs, and Kennard saw the briefest glimpse of what he thought was a forked tongue.

DESPITE HER SERPENTINE APPEARANCE, Kennard had to admit Yakshi was beautiful. Strikingly so. And he could totally believe the folklore of her luring men with her beauty alone. But there was something amiss. There was a darkness to her golden eyes that felt familiar, and as she spoke to Alec, it took a moment for Kennard to realize what it was.

It was sadness.

Manasa shot him a look. "You," she said, her voice like chimes in the wind. "What is your name?"

"I am Kennard, elder of London," he replied.

She smiled and looked to Stas. "Your mate," she said, and a flash of something glinted in the gold of her eyes.

"Yes," Kennard replied.

Manasa looked then at Eiji and Jodis, then between Cronin and Alec. "You are all fated couples."

The snakes in the room became restless, uneasy. They slithered faster, they hissed angrily.

"Yes," Alec answered cautiously. "Is that something that offends you?"

She flinched and then frowned. "No. Apologies. It has been a long time since I have had company."

"May I ask how long?" Alec pressed. He looked around the room at the riches, at the snakes. "I uh, I have a lot of questions."

"Alec always asks a lot of questions," Cronin said with a smile. "A trait that drove me mad when we first met."

Cronin was aiming for humor and an icebreaker, and it

worked. Manasa gave him a small smile. "You came with the intent to harm me," she said, eyeing Alec but with a sly smile. The snakes were calm again, so Kennard assumed her words held no malice. "Your friends here are armed with iron spikes."

"We were unsure of your intent," Alec answered. "Or what we would face when we got here."

"You found all the split gates, and you went through the correct doorways," she said. "You really are the key."

"I am," Alec answered. "None of my friends could see the way here. Only me. Yet if we were all touching, they could pass through the gates with me."

"Clever," Manasa said. She was still, eerily so, in a way that Kennard thought came with the passing of a lot of time. Her gaze drew to Kennard again and she smiled. "You are more perceptive than they know."

Kennard felt every eye in the room on him, snakes included. "What do you mean?"

"You understand me," she murmured lyrically.

"I think you've been here for a long time," Kennard said. "Isolated and alone."

The snakes grew restless again. "The passing of time is lost," she replied. She trailed her pointer finger along the air in front of her. "Yet I can recall every second that I've been here."

"Who put you here?" Jodis asked gently. "If you've been held here against your will, we can help you leave."

The snakes hissed in unison, some raised up, the cobras' hoods fanned out as if ready to strike. Manasa raised a hand and the snakes calmed. "I have spent so long with these creatures, they have become attuned to me." She smiled sadly at the snakes around her feet. "And I to them, I suppose."

Attuned? Kennard thought. *They became part of her!*

After a moment of awkward silence, Alec said, "Manasa, you said you'd been waiting for me. Do you require my help to leave?"

She frowned and the snakes began to sway. "I require your presence..."

"If you've been trapped here, how did you know about the key?" Kennard asked when it was clear Manasa wasn't going to continue. Then, instead of asking her how she fed or if she could never leave or how she had survived this long, he approached from a different angle. "The one who keeps you here," he said. "They hold something over you."

She swayed her head, much like the snakes themselves. "I have been here for many, many years. I do not feed." She put her hand to her throat; gold on gold. "Since I have taken this form, my body requires no sustenance."

It wasn't the question Kennard asked out loud, but the one in his mind that she answered. Then a gold snake slithered to her, wrapping itself around her leg and, as the mercury snakes had done, melded into her body. It became part of her. She swayed her head again, held out her hand toward a crate of golden amulets and necklaces, and a gold snake formed out of her palm and slithered onto the golden treasure.

Kennard risked a glance at Alec and Cronin, who both looked as disturbed as he felt, and Stas slipped his hand into Kennard's. Something wasn't right and Kennard was glad he wasn't the only one who felt it.

"You were not always... golden?" Alec asked.

She swayed her head again. "No." Then she frowned and the snakes were deathly still, all raised up and facing them. "Which of you has gold coins in your pocket?"

Jodis reached into her jeans pocket and produced the

coins. "We found these in the chambers under the Pyramid of the Serpent. Through the split gates. There was also jewelry from Egypt and maybe Mayan or Aztec."

Manasa smiled and peered at the coins Jodis held out. "Ah yes. I remember those."

"Did someone steal them from you?" Alec asked.

Manasa's head shot up to stare at Alec. "Everyone wants to steal from me," she whispered, hiss-like, and the snakes around them hissed in return.

Alec looked her right in the eye. "Not us. That is not why we're here."

"Why *are* you here?" she asked.

"There have been news reports saying the humans are going to open this vault," Alec replied. "We heard rumors of a vampire who guards the vault, and from our past experience in Egypt and China, rumors and folklore always have some origin in fact."

Manasa hummed and the snakes calmed down. "Humans have tried many times—many, many times—to steal from me. They will not breach the doors."

"They don't intend to recite the snake charm," Jodis said. "But to dismantle the temple."

Manasa's gaze hardened and the snakes became uneasy. "The snake charm... what do you know of it?"

"Nothing," Jodis answered. "Only that no human can recite it, and it is the only thing that will open the gates to the vault."

Manasa shook her head. "They must not recite that chant."

Kennard knew there was something Manasa wasn't telling them. If she was unable to say it or bound not to, he didn't know. "It isn't you who we should fear, is it?" Kennard asked. "All the rumors and folklores said that it was the vampire who guards the gold vault who will wreak havoc. But it's not you, is it? Who holds you here, Manasa? Who keeps you hostage? What do they hold over you?"

Manasa bared her fangs and the snakes at her feet all fled, slithering away to hide in the mounds of treasure. "You know more than you're letting on," she hissed. "It is not the key who can see, but you."

Kennard shook his head. "No. I have no powers. I have no vampire talent at all."

"None of us have powers," Alec said. "As soon as we went through the first split gate, we lost our abilities. But Kennard has no extra vampire abilities. Out of all of us, he's the only one who doesn't..." Alec's words died away and he turned slowly to look at Kennard. "Unless in this dimension he does."

Kennard shook his head. "I don't feel any different. I can't leap or replicate, if that's what you're wondering. And thanks for mentioning my absolute lack of talent. Way to make a guy feel special."

"I can get a read on your mind," Manasa said, frowning at Kennard. "But you know something also, don't you?"

Kennard shook his head again. "I don't know what you mean."

"Where did your human life end?" Manasa asked, her snakes hissing at him.

Kennard swallowed hard, not comfortable with her attention. "London."

"Where? Specifically," Manasa furthered. The snakes all reappeared and slithered out, hissing and moving angrily.

Kennard had never told anyone where his human life had ended. He'd admitted the dates and the city, but never the exact location. "The Tower of London."

Manasa hissed, reacting almost violently. "You cannot fool me as you have fooled your friends. You see me as a rightful king sees another of royal blood."

"A rightful king?" Alec asked, risking a glance at Kennard.

"What is she talking about?" Cronin asked. "I've known you the longest, have I not?"

Kennard gave a nod to Cronin, then stared at Manasa. "Fate chose a different life for me."

Jodis studied Kennard for a long moment. "Kennard, what is she talking about? And why did you not dispute her claim?"

Kennard raised his chin and took strength from being close to Stas. "I was born into the English royal family," he whispered.

"*Sangre azul*," Manasa hissed. "It cannot be."

Of course Cronin joined the dots first. "And you died in the Tower of London? Kennard, in 1488..."

Kennard gave him a small smile. "A monarchist to the very end."

Jodis gasped quietly, her eyes wide. "The Princes of the Tower..."

Kennard met her gaze. "Were my brothers. History would go on to say we were killed in 1483, yet we were held for five more winters of hell on earth. Actually, history would have you believe I was never born." Kennard frowned at the human memories he'd tried so hard to forget. "I was the firstborn of twins to Richard and Elizabeth, yet I was born with a poor heart. Ironically, a condition fixed by my human death. Being a sickly child, I was never intended for greatness, hidden from public record. My twin brother was supposed to take the title, yet our uncle saw to our end."

"Kennard, you are..." Cronin whispered.

"The rightful heir to the throne," Manasa finished. She hissed angrily. "Royal blood."

"Any hold on that title was stripped from me with my humanity," Kennard replied. "Even as a human, I was never destined for the throne."

"Yet the bloodline remains," Manasa said, and the snakes in the room hissed.

Eiji blinked, then blinked again. "Kennard..." He gawped at Jodis but pointed to Kennard. "Is King of *England*?"

Stas looked at Kennard, confused. "You not tell me?"

"Because it's not something I care to remember, and the title was not ever to be mine," Kennard whispered. "I was a poorly infant who somehow lived long enough to be a poorly child, thrown into a dungeon cell. Too weak to fight to protect my brothers." He shook his head, sadly. "My uncle made a deal with a vampire who could influence behaviors. He convinced parliament that we were illegitimate children not eligible for the crown, and he rose to power quickly. My uncle took the throne and handed over three young princes as payment." Kennard lifted his chin. "The vampire kept us imprisoned, and he... enjoyed... my brothers first, and by some cruel hand of fate, I survived."

Stas put his huge hand to Kennard's face. "Not cruel hand. You survived for me. To make complete me."

Kennard smiled at his broken English and kissed his palm. Then he turned to the golden vampire. "Manasa, I promise you, I see no more than anyone else," he said. He turned to Alec. "Well, apart from the fact that she's mad as a bag of ferrets and that she's hiding the truth. But I'm pretty sure anyone with eyes can see that."

All the snakes reacted, raising their head and hissing angrily. Manasa bared her teeth.

But Kennard was done. He felt raw and exposed, having admitted to too much already. He pulled Stas behind him, protecting him from the snakes, took out the iron spike from his pocket, and he noticed that Eiji and Jodis followed his lead. "But I am done with your games, Manasa. Answer the question. Who holds you here?"

Her face twisted with pain, but she said nothing.

"Alec," Kennard said. "Let's go. Leave her here for another thousand years, alone with her own misery and mind games. And if the humans do open this damn vault, let them have all that's within it."

Manasa's fangs gleamed, her beautiful face marred with pain. "I cannot leave," she cried. "For as long as the curse remains. Only the key will set me free."

"From who?" Alec asked.

"Who holds you here?" Kennard asked again. "Did they threaten you?"

Manasa looked at Kennard and a single golden tear ran down her cheek before it simply became part of her face. "She turned my love to gold," she said, looking at the gold statue of the supine man on the bed of snakes. "She holds him hostage in full golden form. I am forced to live this half-life, half alive, half gold until the key comes. She can't escape without you. I'm sorry," she said, looking to Alec. "I'm sorry, but it's the only way she'll give him back to me."

"A name," Kennard demanded. "Give us a name!"

"You know her by many names," Manasa cried. "To the Hindu, she is Nagini. To the Japanese, she is Benzaiten. Aztecs called her Coatlicue."

Then all the snakes slithered to the wall. The golden snakes climbed upward, forming a doorway. Not just any doorway. A split gate. Then the stone snakes formed an inner frame, and as soon as the last snake was in place, a door shimmered into view.

Manasa took a step back, clearly afraid. "She comes now. Please know I am sorry. The key must get the Cintamani stone."

"What is the Cintamani stone?"

Manasa turned to the gateway, to the figure about to enter. "She is here."

Kennard crouched low, ready to strike, as did everyone else. Ready to take on whoever was about to slide through the gateway. The space in the doorway resembled a vertical wall of water and it looked as if there were fish or sharks swimming past on the other side. It took Kennard a moment to realize it didn't look like water. It *was* water.

And then a figure appeared, shimmering and looming before she stepped through the doorway. Kennard couldn't believe what he saw.

A woman, she wore a white Grecian-style dress which was dripping wet, and water now pooled at her feet. Her skin resembled that of a pale shark, her eyes were abnormally round, her irises were vertical slits as well. She was frighteningly ugly. But her hair... her hair was...

She smiled to reveal vampire fangs, and Kennard gasped. In all his years, he'd never seen anything like it.

He knew exactly who she was. They *all* knew.

Her hair wriggled and writhed above her head, disturbing and horrid. Before she could speak, before she could introduce herself, Alec whispered her name.

"Medusa."

CHAPTER SEVEN

MEDUSA PUT her hand to Manasa's cheek. "You're a good pet," she said.

Manasa flinched and cowered a little, and it was very clear that she was afraid of Medusa. Manasa took a step back, her head bowed, her hands clasped in front of her.

Medusa turned her attention to Kennard and the others, noted their defensive stances, and smiled. She looked right at Alec. "The key," she said, and the snakes on her head all faced Alec.

"I am the key. I am Ailig McAidan, the one you seek."

Medusa's gaze hardened at Alec and studied him; the snakes on her head all hissed, their tongues tasting the air. "You do have mercury in your blood. I can smell it." Then she looked at each of the vampires facing her. "A welcoming party. How very Grecian of you." She glided over to the golden snakes who still formed the writhing gateway. She stroked them lovingly.

Eiji crouched in a defensive pose, but Jodis put her hand on his arm, silently urging him not to attack. Cronin gave a slight shake of his head, and Stas moved a fraction in front of Kennard.

"We are not Grecian," Alec said. "We came here because we thought the discovery of the vampire guarding this vault would expose our world. The humans are trying to open it as we speak."

"The humans will fail, as humans always do. The doors they try to open are not the way to enter," Medusa replied simply. She turned to look at them now, smiling, her hair slithering about her head. She studied Stas for a moment, the biggest of them all. "You stand to protect the one behind you."

Stas gave a nod, and Kennard could feel him tense. He felt his unease and fear. "Always," Stas said.

Medusa looked back to Kennard. "Then who are you?"

"I am Kennard, Elder of London," he replied.

"An elder. I'm honored," she said, though it was said with both contempt and sarcasm. She smiled up at Stas. "And you must be his mate?"

"I am," he replied.

"They are all mated pairs," Manasa said weakly.

"That's good to know," Medusa replied, giving Manasa a quick glance. "Leverage is a powerful weapon."

"I've done my part," Manasa replied. She stepped forward. "I've done as you asked. Now it is your turn to—"

Medusa raised a hand. "I will say when your part here is done."

Manasa was tearful. "You promised—"

"Our agreement is not complete yet," Medusa replied.

"You said when the key is found— all I had to do was lure him here," Manasa tried. Her change in demeanor, going from bad guy to victim, didn't sit well with Kennard.

"I am not free yet," Medusa replied. She waved her

hand around the golden room. "I can go no farther than here. Confined to this realm for all eternity. This room and my ocean kingdom through there, of course." She smiled to the doorway of water. "Confined for millennia until the key could unlock the gates to set me free."

"Ocean kingdom?" Jodis asked. She glanced to the doorway of vertical water. "So it is true. May I touch it?"

Kennard wondered what Jodis' ploy was in asking, but perhaps Jodis knew something he didn't. This meeting hadn't gone entirely pear-shaped yet—despite him having divulged far more information than he'd ever intended—so maybe keeping this meeting amicable or keeping Medusa distracted was Jodis' intent.

"What's your name?" Medusa asked.

"I am Jodis," she replied serenely. "I have heard much about you, but I was led to believe it all a myth." She stepped closer to Medusa. "You are a Gorgon, the queen of the sea."

"A sea daemon," Medusa said. "Vampires that can live in water or on land."

Jodis turned back to Alec and said, "Gorgon is a Greek word that lends from Sanskrit, the language of ancient India." Jodis turned back to Medusa and smiled. "You'll have to forgive my curiosity, we were led to believe the last of the Gorgoneia coven was killed thousands of years ago."

"I am the last," Medusa said. "Banished. Until now."

Jodis waved her hand toward the water door. "Is this, your ocean kingdom, what I think it is?"

Medusa smiled again and the snakes around her head swayed with ease. She held out her hand and Jodis took it. Kennard risked a glance to Eiji and Alec, and they seemed as perplexed as he was. Together the two women walked hand in hand to the shimmering doorway of water.

"This is Atlantis," Jodis said. It wasn't a question. She put her hand up but didn't touch the water. "You said you were confined here? Banished?"

Medusa made a distasteful sound and her snakes became agitated. Kennard saw Eiji hesitate, but Alec slowly reached out and held Eiji's arm. When Eiji shot him a look, Alec shook his head.

"My sisters were murdered and I was taken by Poseidon and his Aegean coven. They covered my eyes so I could not turn them to stone," Medusa said quietly, the snakes at her head hissing.

"You are a mason," Jodis said with a slight laugh. "The myth is true. You can turn things to stone."

Medusa ran her fingers along one of the stone snakes at the doorway. "Yes. When I want."

"And Poseidon...," Jodis prompted.

"He did... unspeakable things," she replied, her snakes hissing in response. "They all did."

Aegean. Poseidon. Atlantis... Kennard couldn't believe what he was hearing.

Medusa's snakes writhed angrily. "Poseidon's mate, Athena, blamed me for what he did and she banished me here. A world in between, neither here nor there. Damned for all eternity in the waters of Acheron in Atlantis. Or Ancient Dwarka. Avalon, Lemuria. Whatever culture, whichever you'd like to call it."

"Dwarka is an underwater Indian city, supposedly full of gold," Jodis said, Kennard assumed, for their benefit.

"The ancient worlds are connected, one and the same," Medusa said. "Religions, myths, folklore. Humans are so concerned with labels. All myths and legends come from history, do they not? It depends on one's beliefs what they are prepared to admit as fact or fiction."

"I am sorry they mistreated you. The Aegean coven," Jodis said. "I hope they paid for it."

Medusa smiled in such a horrific way, Kennard suppressed a shudder. "Dearly," Medusa said. "They all stand as stone statues in my water kingdom."

"Good, I'm glad," Jodis said, pleasing Medusa. "May I touch the water?" Jodis asked once more.

"If you so wish."

"Jodis," Eiji whispered in warning.

Jodis smiled at Medusa. "He worries harm will come to me if I touch it."

Medusa eyed Eiji for a moment; her snakes writhed in his direction, but she turned back to Jodis and smiled. "No harm will come. You have my word."

Jodis lifted her fingers to the edge of the shimmering water wall, and ever so delicately, her fingertips sank into the surface. "So remarkable," she murmured. "May I be so bold as to ask if we can enter?" Jodis asked Medusa before giving Eiji and Alec a look Kennard couldn't quite read.

Medusa eyed her for a long second. Her snakes grew restless. "Your purpose?"

"It's not every day we can say we visited the lost city of Atlantis." Jodis withdrew her fingers from the water and smiled serenely at her. "To see such a thing would be a great honor."

Medusa looked back at the vampires watching, and her gaze landed on Alec. "Yes, I should like very much for you to see my city."

Jodis gave Alec a pointed stare and a hard nod, which he read without letting on. "Yes, thank you," Alec said. "We would be honored."

Kennard stared at Alec. "We would?"

Alec hardened his eyes and nodded to the doorway of water, not very subtly. "Yes, apparently we would."

Jodis covered with a laugh. "Come on, boys. Hurry along."

Kennard shook his head with disbelief and slipped out of his jacket, dropping it at his feet. He lifted one foot and began unbuckling and untying the laces. "And if you think I'm wearing three thousand dollar boots into the ocean..."

Manasa skittered over to Medusa. "You will return, yes?" She was upset, almost frantic. "You still have your promise to keep."

"I will keep my end of the bargain," Medusa said. "But first I want to show the key my kingdom."

Kennard didn't like the way she said that, and from the dubious glance she got from Cronin, Kennard wasn't the only one. Kennard could feel the unease coming from Stas, so he put his hand on his arm. "We'll be okay. It's just water."

Jodis sighed and crossed the room to Eiji. She held out her hand, palm downward, which Eiji took immediately. When she pulled her hand away, Kennard could see what she'd given Eiji. It was ice.

"Come on, boys. Must you be late for everything?" Jodis said as she pulled Eiji toward the door, toward Medusa.

Alec smiled now and followed them both with Cronin right behind him. Kennard grinned at Stas and took his hand, feeling hugely relieved. Everything Jodis had done now made sense, her whole ruse to touch the water and perhaps even her kindness toward Medusa. Jodis had just discovered something that would give them an advantage.

Ice.

If Jodis could produce ice from the water of Atlantis, it

meant once they went through the water gateway, everyone would have their powers back.

"Uh, first, before we enter," Cronin said. "Kennard, our conversation about you and England is far from over."

Kennard sighed. "I assumed as much."

They stood at the vertical wall of water, and Jodis entered first. Then Eiji, Alec, and Cronin. Kennard, still holding Stas' hand, took a deep breath for luck and stepped inside.

Into Atlantis.

KENNARD COULD BARELY REMEMBER the last time he'd been swimming. There was that time in Whitechapel, in 1888, when he and a few of his London coven had hidden their tracks by jumping into the Thames. Jack the Ripper had made such a terrible mess, the cleanup—to cover up all trace of vampire and make it look as human as possible—had been quite problematic at the time. Bloodhounds had tracked them back to a coven-owned house and risked exposing them, so they needed to divert the scent. Leading them away and into the Thames had put an end to the local bobby's suspicions. For a short while, anyway. Not that the Thames was exactly a pleasant swim.

Not like this.

Atlantis was crystal clear, layers of blue upon blue for as far as he could see. Vampires were adept at swimming; holding one's breath wasn't difficult when they didn't need to breathe, so Kennard had no doubt Stas would be fine but it didn't stop him from checking. He turned to Stas who was just a foot or so behind him. His short hair bristled in the water, bubbles of oxygen clung to his skin, and his eyes sparkled. A bubble escaped him as he grinned.

Kennard wanted to test Jodis' theory.

Can you hear me, Stas?

He grinned wider and gave a nod.

Can you all hear me? It was Alec's voice. *Don't act like you can hear me. Just go along with me for now.*

Seemingly oblivious to their silent conversation, Medusa swam ahead, fast and serpent-like. Her snake hair writhed fluidly, and her skin looked iridescent in the water. She was a Gorgon, Kennard reminded himself. A sea daemon. She was stronger when underwater.

She turned toward the vast emptiness of water, then as if she was conducting an orchestra, Medusa waved her hands and mountains of stone appeared before them.

No, not mountains. Temples. A temple identical to Angkor Wat appeared, brick by brick, layer by layer, built up from a sea-bottom that Kennard couldn't see. Complete with serpent gargoyles that moved and slithered along their stone confines.

She hadn't built it right before their eyes, Kennard realized. She'd revealed it.

Holy fucking shit. Alec cursed.

Medusa turned to them and smiled, proud, gloating. "Invisible to those who aren't worthy of seeing it," she said. Her ability to speak underwater must have been born from thousands of years of practice.

"It's beautiful," Jodis replied, sounding warbled and bubbly.

And that would be why no human has ever found it, Alec added.

Kennard looked back at the way they had come, and gave Alec a mental nod to what he saw. At the end of the stone courtyard was a stone split gate. The other side of the gate seemed to drop away into the depth of the ocean.

"There is no surface above. No shore, no air," Medusa said, waving her hand upward. "There is only endless ocean. Believe me, I've spent millennia searching for a way out."

Jesus Christ. Alec's mental exclamation matched Kennard's own.

"Come this way," Medusa said, swimming toward the first temple doorway.

The reflex to inhale was so ingrained, Kennard had to make the conscious effort not to. He had no idea what they were about to face inside the temple, but he was certainly not expecting what he found.

The room opened up like a great hall, like the stone churches that had graced Kennard's beloved England hundreds of years ago. Only this was round, circular like the Tholos of Delphi. It was a temple. A squared platform was raised in the middle and a throne sat in its center. Large, made of stone, carved with serpents. Cobras with extended hoods framed the backrest, and Kennard didn't need to ask who the throne belonged to. Medusa twirled in the grand space as though some macabre music played that only she could hear.

Though it had a definite Greek or Roman look, or maybe that was because of who was in it. Because at the sides of the grand hall, like pillars, stood the stone statues—the stone bodies, rather—of those history had claimed had wronged her.

Poseidon.

Athena.

Hades.

Demeter.

Apollo.

Holy shit. She'd turned them to stone and kept them, like grisly trophies. She'd decorated her home with them. Hell, she'd just danced between their dead, stone bodies.

"They got what they deserved," she declared as though she was commenting on oil paintings instead of marble corpses. The snakes around her head writhed, and Kennard wasn't sure if it was the water or if they danced with her happiness. "Poseidon built this city for Athena," Medusa said, running her finger down Athena's dress. "They lured me here to do what they did. And now it belongs to me." Medusa looked at the stone statues, then back to Kennard and his friends. She gave a sinister smile. "Now they belong to me."

She then swam like a sea snake over to the throne. But she didn't sit in it. She stood beside it.

Something was wrong. A queen, even self-appointed, would always take the throne. Unless she wasn't the ruling monarch. Unless someone else ruled the kingdom...

Alec, something's not right, Kennard said mentally. *We need to leave.*

But Alec wasn't looking. He was staring at the floor of the temple, under their feet, and it made Kennard look too. In the circular temple floor was carved a triangle, from one edge of the circle to the other, and within that was the squared platform, and atop that the throne. Which sat in the center of a circle, carved into the stone.

Alec looked at Medusa. He shook his head. "This is a squared circle."

"Very good," Medusa replied. "You are indeed the key to me. The key that will reopen all the gates to this world. Ailig McAidan, you are the Magnum Opus."

The what? *The greatest work?* What the...?

Before Kennard could ask this out loud, Alec spun to look behind them. Then, as she did before, like conducting an orchestra, Medusa waved her hands and another stone monument took form. At first Kennard thought they were many pillars, another temple perhaps. But a grislier form took shape. It was an enormous cage with a stone beast confined within its walls.

Not just any beast. It looked like all the stone statues they'd seen all over Malaysia and Indonesia, in Mayan pyramids, in Buddhist temples. Like the paintings they'd seen in Japan, China, Egypt. Except it was huge. The size of three double-decker buses. It was a dragon-like snake with ferocious looking teeth and fangs. And in the middle of its forehead was a large red stone.

"Do you know what this is?" Medusa asked, her voice in a singsong.

"Puff, the Magic Dragon?" Alec answered.

The snakes around Medusa's head all hissed and she snarled. "This is Makara." Medusa swam to the stone bars of the cage, swimming in and out of them before stopping in front of Alec. "He is a sea dragon, belonging to Varuna or Poseidon, whatever you want to call him. Every culture has a different name for the same thing."

"If you turned Makara to stone, why is he caged?" Alec asked.

"Because in the stone body, the creature yet lives," she replied cheerfully.

"You've kept him alive only to imprison him in a stone body?" Eiji asked. "So he cannot move? Or swim? Or feed? What kind of fresh hell is that?"

Medusa's gaze shot to Eiji for a long moment before she answered his questions with a nonchalant shrug. Kennard had no idea what Alec saw in her mind, but he put his hand on Eiji's arm, warning enough to not anger her.

"I have kept him alive all this time, as I have kept all of them alive," she said, waving her hand to the stone statues of Poseidon and his coven. "So they can witness my success. Waiting for the key. I need Alec to remove the stone from Makara. I have tried but I cannot. Only the key can remove it."

Jesus. All those statues were alive? Imprisoned in their own bodies but fully aware of what was going on around them, happening to them. Kennard couldn't imagine a fate worse than death. Until now.

Cronin looked to Alec. "Why the red stone? What's so special about it?"

"It's the Cintamani stone," Alec answered. "The Hindu people call it the Cintamani stone. Though it has a few names. Parasmani stone. Angelicall Stone. But we know it as the philosopher's stone."

The philosopher's... "You're kidding, right?" Kennard asked.

"Not kidding." Alec shook his head. "Medusa's throne sits on a squared circle, which looks a helluva lot like the deathly hallows. And I tell ya, when all this shit is done, J.K. Rowling and I are gonna sit down and have ourselves a little chat."

CHAPTER EIGHT

MEDUSA WAS ELATED, as though her dreams were all coming true. Her sinister smile, the way her snakes danced about her head gave Kennard the creeps. "Yes," Medusa said. "The stone belonged to Kubera. You might know him as Midas."

Midas...

Medusa waved her hand to one of the stone statues in her circle temple. Kennard followed her line of sight to a statue with a long beard and with his hand extended into the depth of water that surrounded him.

Fucking hell... Is that actually Midas?

Alec gave him a small nod.

"A stone that can turn anything to gold," Medusa said. "How else do you think the Golden Temple of India came to be?"

The stone...

"If it turns things to gold, how can it help you leave Atlantis?" Kennard asked.

"Because it is also the elixir of life," Alec answered instead. "It allows anyone who holds it immortality."

"I do not need immortality," Medusa said. Her smile was creepy; her snakes were writhing happily. "I need it to open the gates so I may walk the earth once more."

"I'm not sure I can do that," Alec said.

She swam toward him, fast and slippery. Eerily. She stopped, her face just a few inches from Alec's, her round eyes staring, unblinking. "Can't or won't?" Medusa asked.

Alec smiled at her, and suddenly, Medusa went still, as though she'd been frozen in time. Even her snake hair was still, unmoving in the water.

Alec took a step back and shook his head. "I've had enough of her games. She's batshit fucking crazy."

Eiji laughed, but Jodis shook her head, frowning. "She has her reasons," Jodis replied. "They did unspeakable things to her and left her here in this underwater prison. Only she fought back and imprisoned them instead."

Alec conceded with a nod. "True. I know she has her reasons, but her intent is to cause further harm. She's unstable, and even if she did make it back to the real world, the vampire elder council would stop her. She would expose everyone without care or concern. I can see it in her mind, and I can see the future she wants."

"What did you do to her?" Cronin asked, staring at Medusa's still form. "Is she dead, or just..."

"She's not dead," he replied. "Not yet." Alec turned to the stone dragon. "We need to figure out what to do with this guy, then with Poseidon and his coven."

"Leave them here," Eiji said. "But put them out of their misery first."

"I agree," Kennard said, and Stas nodded his agreement.

"Her mind," Stas said, "is not a good place. No happiness. Only resentment and revenge." He eyed Medusa.

"Her story is a sad one, but if it not end today, it will not end well for anyone."

Alec agreed. "She's been put through enough. I think they all have." He then put his hand to Medusa's forehead. "May you find peace," he said, and then, as if her body petrified from the inside out, she turned to stone. Then Alec turned to the circle of Poseidon and his coven and threw out his hands. Kennard could see the change in the statues. Their eyes seemed to harden even more and there was almost a collective sigh of relief from them as Alec ended their millennia of imprisonment.

Then he swam to Makara, the stone dragon. Alec ran his hand over the creature's brow as though he were having a silent conversation with it, and just as Kennard thought he was about to put the animal out of its misery, Alec spun around to look at the way they had come. His face filled with shock and horror.

Kennard turned to see the shimmer of something gold flash through the water before it disappeared—something incredibly huge and serpent-like—and the next thing he knew, they were all on their asses in the Golden Temple.

THEY ALL STRUGGLED TO BREATHE, gasping for air and coughing up water. They were all drenched, sopping wet, their hair flat down their faces, their clothes sticking to their bodies, sitting in the room of gold.

Everyone except Alec.

Alec wasn't there.

"Alec! Alec!" Cronin cried. He looked around the room frantically, then scrambled to his feet and ran to where the shimmering door of water had been, where it was no longer.

The gateway into Atlantis was gone and in its place was only stone. A sob tore from Cronin and he put his hand to his heart. "M'cridhe. M'graidh..." He crumpled, leaning on the wall for support, and Kennard could barely compute what was happening. Cronin gasped a breath and sobbed. "I can't feel him."

Alec? No, Alec can't really be gone...

Jodis and Eiji started to go to him but stopped halfway. She had her hand out to Cronin, and Eiji put his hand on her arm as though it was helpless; what could they possibly do? The utter silence was deafening. The pain radiating from Cronin was heartbreaking...

If Alec was gone, Cronin would soon follow. No mate could survive the loss. No mate would want to.

Kennard put his hand to his mouth, his eyes filled with tears, and he reached for Stas. He needed his touch, he needed his comfort. Stas pulled him in close and held him tight. Then he went still.

Kennard looked up at him. "Stas, what is it?"

"Cronin!" Stas jumped to his feet and ran to Cronin. "I hear him. I can hear him in my mind. Alec, he is alive."

Cronin looked up at Stas, devastation turning to hope. "You can?"

Stas nodded, and relief detonated in the room. "Only faint. But is him."

Cronin gripped Stas' arm. "Can you speak to him? Can he see me through your eyes?"

Stas went still again, then he nodded. "It be faint, but yes. His powers are strong."

Cronin clenched his teeth, fangs out, and pointed his finger at the wall. "Then tell him to open this fucking door. Alec, you open this goddamn door. *Sa mhionaid! Damataidh*, Ailig!"

Kennard knew when Cronin broke out in Scottish Gaelic his emotions were running high. Also, when the veins in his neck and forehead popped out, it was never good.

Stas grimaced and made an apologetic face. "He said, No take that tone with him."

Cronin growled, stepping in close, and stared back at Stas. "Alec," he growled. "You come back to me. Now."

Kennard was quick to stand in front of Stas. He knew Cronin was torn, but Kennard's instinct to protect Stas was overwhelming.

"Is okay," Stas said calmly, his huge hand on Kennard's neck. "He speak to Alec, not me."

"Uh, guys," Eiji said. "I hate to bring this up, and Cronin, I'm sure Alec will be fine. And Kennard, we will discuss the whole king thing. But Manasa, the vampire who guarded this gold room?" He gestured broadly to the room. "Manasa? She's not here."

"She is in there," Stas said, nodding to the wall. "She is big snake that Alec fight."

"Big snake?" Kennard and Cronin asked in unison.

"Alec call her basa... something." Stas squinted and shook his head. "Hard to understand. He move too fast. Basa... lisk?"

"The basilisk?" everyone cried.

"What do you mean he moves too fast?" Cronin asked.

Stas made a face. "He hides from the basilisk. He blinks in and out, leaping. So basilisk gaze not touch him."

"A basilisk can kill with just a look," Jodis said quietly.

"Why can't Alec just freeze it or turn it to stone? Or make it explode?" Eiji asked. "Alec can do these things. Or catch fire. Like the couch that time."

"A basilisk is immune. It can only be killed one way,"

Jodis said. Everyone stared at her waiting... "The eye of Medusa."

"Too late for that," Cronin cried. "He just killed her."

"There is another way," Kennard said. "Geoffrey Chaucer mentions the basilisk."

"Who?" Eiji asked.

"Geoffrey Chaucer," Kennard answered, duly offended. "Who happens to be the grandfather of English literature."

"What did he say?" Cronin asked, his patience run thin.

"In the Canterbury Tales, he says the creature can be killed with a mirror. To see itself would kill it."

They looked around the room of golden treasure, at mountains of coins, goblets, statues, jewelry. Eiji ran to the closest mound and began to dismantle it, only finding more coins and goblets and jewelry underneath. Cronin shook his head. "There would be no mirrors here. If Manasa was truly the basilisk all along, there's no way she'd have a mirror here."

"Cronin's right," Jodis said.

"We need to get in there. Now," Cronin barked. "We must help him."

Stas nodded but squinted again and put his hand up. "Alec say if we go back to Atlantis, we not come back here."

"Yes. Anything. Whatever it takes," Cronin answered quickly.

Jodis nodded. "We cannot leave this room without Alec anyway. Our powers don't work here and it is completely sealed. We have to go back."

Eiji gave Cronin a sad smile. "You need to be with Alec, and if it is your fate to go back to Atlantis, then it is ours as well. If we are doomed to spend eternity in Atlantis, we do it together."

Kennard slid his arm around Stas and gave Cronin a nod. "Musketeers and all that."

"*Tapadh leat.*" Cronin gave them a teary nod, then he looked up at Stas. "Alec, m'cridhe. Can you leap us in there? Please."

After a moment, Stas gave a nod. "He say yes."

And in the next blink of an eye, they were all back in the depths of Atlantis. Alec had delivered them around Makara, the stone dragon. The five of them at equal points in formation, Kennard quickly deduced, to defend it. They trod water in the vastness of blue ocean and they each watched in horror as the huge basilisk slithered before them. Rising above them, her forked tongue and fangs hid her smile.

Alec blinked into view at the fore, between them and the serpent. "Do not look at her! Do not make eye contact!" he said. He floated, treading water in front of the basilisk. "She needs the stone."

She hissed. The sound reverberated through the water, a piercing sound that made Kennard and the others cover their ears before the sound died away, leaving his ears aching. Then she zeroed in on him. Her focus solely on Kennard, she writhed in the water, darting toward him. Alec and Stas, obviously seeing her intentions, were suddenly in front of Kennard. Stas held his iron spike in one hand, his other in a fist, and he roared at her. It was a frightening sight. She was bigger than him, but his rage at her intent to harm Kennard made Stas seem like a mountain.

Alec was suspended in the water next to Stas, a united front. "You will not harm him," Alec said.

Manasa hissed, a taunting smile on her serpent mouth. Her forked tongue goaded them. "What does she want to kill me for?" Kennard asked. "What threat am I to her?"

"I don't know," Alec said. "Her mind is only anger. Whatever you do, do not make eye contact." Then Alec threw out a shield, a barrier between Manasa and them. "I doubt that will hold her back. Nothing else has worked."

"Alec, you need a mirror," Cronin cried. "To kill her."

He shook his head. "I can't leap anything physical in from the outside world. Not even the metaphysical can hold her."

"Your mirrors won't work in the waters of Atlantis," the basilisk said, Manasa's voice hissing. "And your mind tricks don't work on me either. I'm protected in Atlantis. Why do you think Medusa kept me out of here? You should have killed me in the gold prison when you had your chance."

"Manasa," Alec tried. "I don't want to have to kill you."

"Kill me?" she laughed. "Don't you see what you've done? The key, the great vampire savior has set me free. I didn't need the royal's blood after all. The key killed Medusa. The one who kept me locked in that golden prison," she said, her voice papery. "And now Makara and the stone. You have set me free! I will rise once more in flooded waters and claim what is rightfully mine."

"What is with these freaks and world domination?" Eiji said.

She hissed again, louder this time, and Kennard had to cover his ears. The sound pierced through his brain. Kennard felt as if the sound could actually kill him.

Alec threw out his hands and roared, "I don't speak Parseltongue, bitch." Plumes of waves left his hands and pushed the basilisk backward, pummeling her in the water. But she wasn't hindered for long. She slithered backwards, her long body gliding faster through the water than Kennard could have thought possible. She flicked her tail, causing shock waves to push back, and they each had to grab onto Makara, the stone dragon, so they didn't float away.

Kennard grabbed Makara's ear and the stone in the center of its forehead caught his eye.

She can't get the stone if it doesn't exist.

Hearing Kennard's thought, Alec shot him a look. "Keep her busy," Kennard said, and he took out the iron spike Eiji had given him. Holding it in his fist, he stabbed the stone.

Manasa's shrill hiss pierced the water and everyone recoiled. "Quick!" Alec cried.

He must have given them all a mental plan because Jodis, Cronin, and Eiji suddenly blinked out of view. Stas and Alec stood guard in front of Kennard. Kennard tried to smash the stone again, but the iron spike had no impact.

He turned to see Cronin, Eiji, and Jodis all blink in and out of view around Manasa's long body. They stabbed at her with their iron spikes and she thrashed wildly, hissing that awful keening sound that threatened to split Kennard's skull. The superficial wounds weren't going to be fatal to Manasa, but they sure did make her angry.

"I thought iron was supposed to hurt her?" Eiji yelled. She swung her head around toward him.

"Watch her eyes!" Alec yelled. Jodis threw out her hand, sending a spear of ice through Manasa's body before she could reach Eiji.

Manasa screamed and thrashed, but the ice soon melted in the water and Manasa's wound healed over. Jodis did it again and again, all along her long serpent body, even through her head, but nothing was killing her.

"I've tried everything," Alec said. "She's immune to my powers."

"The stone!" Kennard yelled, trying in vain to smash it.

"The secret is in the stone. It's what she wants. But I can't break it."

Stas took his iron spike and tried to smash the stone, to no avail. Stas, the strongest vampire Kennard had ever met... if he couldn't do it...

He tried again but missed, and the iron spike stuck the stone instead. It crumbled a little, and so he did it again, and Kennard did it too, but then Alec appeared beside them. He touched Makara's face and the dragon crumbled to dust, and the stone flew into Alec's waiting hand.

"Couldn't have done the whole Jedi thing sooner?" Kennard asked.

Alec probably would have laughed if right then Manasa hadn't gone absolutely ballistic.

ALEC LEAPT, blinking in and out of view, to go from where Kennard had been to the throne that stood atop the squared circle. "Alec, what are you doing?" Cronin yelled. He leapt so fast, repeatedly stabbing Manasa, Kennard could hardly make out where his voice was coming from. He could only see the swirls of water Alec left in his wake.

"I'm putting an end to her," Alec replied.

Manasa now focused on Alec. He kept his gaze away, never making eye contact with her. He held out his hand with the philosopher's stone. "My powers do work in here. Not against her directly, but this should do the trick."

Manasa hissed, baring her fangs, and slowly began to swim toward him. "What are you doing?" she asked, her tone alarmed and shrill.

Kennard didn't know whether it was Alec or Cronin

who leapt them, but they all now found themselves standing behind Alec.

"We're in the squared circle," Alec said. "A symbol in alchemy long thought to reflect the interplay of the philosopher's stone. But I'm guessing that's not it at all. I'll bet anything it's to destroy it."

Manasa hissed, an eardrum piercing sound. "You won't dare!"

"Watch me," he answered. He pointed to Poseidon's trident. "He holds the answer. The trident is the answer. The three primes, the *tria prima* we need are sulfur, salt, and mercury. The ocean provides two of them, and I can't leap anything in from the outside world, but I can use what's here." Alec reached out and squeezed a handful of water in his fist, as though he was taking a hold of a physical thing, only when he opened his hand, he had a handful of white and yellow crystals: salt and sulfur. He poured them over the philosopher's stone. "And I provide the third. Mercury." Smiling, Alec put his hand to his mouth and bit, piercing the skin. He rubbed the droplets of blood onto the sulfur and the philosopher's stone.

Everyone waited, and on the far wall, a shimmering door began to appear. A door, a gateway started to take shape. Manasa laughed and slithered happily in the water. "Thank you, key."

Alec jerked back and shook his head, horrified. "No. It was supposed to kill her. Not open the door!"

But Kennard could see. It all made sense in his head now. He could see what he needed to do. It was why Manasa had been so interested in his bloodline.

What did Manasa call him? *Sangre azul.* Kennard knew those words...

Blue blood.

His bloodline was blue.

He swam for Alec. *Do you trust me?*

Alec gave a nod and handed Kennard the philosopher's stone. He bit into his own hand, then held the stone with that hand, letting the stone sit in his blood. He remembered words spoken from his human days. "A vial of sacred blood."

At first nothing happened, and Kennard might have thought it hadn't worked either, but Manasa's shrill laughter morphed into a hiss, then became more of a scream. Then she began to swim, slithering around the circular platform, swimming around the throne, around them. Faster and faster until the water became a vortex, yet they were completely still inside it. Kennard didn't know if that was because Alec was protecting them; he assumed it was. Then suddenly a blue flame sparked on Kennard's hand. Then another. Then it combusted and he was holding a ball of blue fire in his hand.

"Yes! Burn! Sacred blood burns the bluest flame," Kennard cried, and Manasa screamed.

Red liquid ran from his hand, through his fingers, and it looked like blood, as if his hand was melting, but then Kennard remembered that sulfur became a red liquid when it heated. The stone, the sulfur, salt, Alec's mercury, and Kennard's blood were melting together. The blue flame on his palm grew bigger, sparking violently, even in the water. It lit up the darkest parts of Atlantis; the whole dimension was eerily blue.

"The four elements," Alec yelled, now understanding. "Fire, water, wind, and stone!"

Kennard grinned as Manasa's screams reached a peak, as did the vortex around them with the height of the blue flame, and when the screaming stopped, the water slowed, and Manasa became ash and she broke apart, floating away around them. The fire died away, all that remained of the philosopher's stone swirling to nothing on Kennard's palm.

They all stood there, each looked at the other, unsure if they should believe it was over. Cronin broke first by swimming over to Alec. "Is it done, m'cridhe?"

Alec gave a nod. "It is done. Kennard, you did it!" He was quick to hug Kennard but let him go just as fast and handed him over to Stas. Alec soon found Cronin's arms and Jodis pulled Eiji in and kissed him, but Kennard was lost to the warmth and safety of Stas' embrace. He felt immediate relief and the instant realization of being complete. He reached up to Stas' face, pulled him in for a kiss, wrapping his legs around him, and Stas deepened the kiss.

Someone cleared their throat. "Uh, guys," Alec said to them. "How about we leave before you two go any further. I already have enough mental images of what Kennard wants Stas to do to him to last me a lifetime."

"What do you mean a lifetime?" Eiji asked Alec, confused. "You're immortal."

Alec gave a grim nod. "Exactly."

Kennard slid down Stas' body. "You're welcome, Alec. And I hate to be the one to bring it up, after the whole alchemy lesson in Poseidon's squared circle of Atlantis and all, but given Manasa's escape doorway didn't form properly, how do we leave exactly?" Kennard waved toward where the gateway into the Golden Temple had been. "Our exit to the real world is gone."

"There's a gateway," Alec said. "The gateway Manasa wanted." But then he stopped. "Wait. I need a souvenir for our wall." He held his hand out toward Poseidon. His trident shook, then snapped free of his stone fist and flew through the water to Alec's waiting hand. "Perfect."

Cronin laughed, and Eiji rolled his eyes, but Kennard took Stas' hand and they followed Alec, swimming down to the stone wall until a shimmering familiar shape appeared in the blue depths. A split gate in the stone wall.

"Of course it is," Kennard said flatly.

Alec laughed and held the trident in his right hand and held his left out to Cronin. "Join hands."

Once they'd formed another vampire chain, Alec slipped through the gate and led them into darkness.

CHAPTER NINE

STILL UNDERWATER, Kennard noticed the change in pressure first, or depth, he realized, then the change in temperature. They were in warmer waters, yes. The pressure in his head and on his body was different. And the water was more green than blue, but the water was still and there were no fish.

Kennard wondered if they would have to go through as many gates to return to the real world as it took them to get to the gold vault and Atlantis. But before he could ask where on earth they were, they rounded a mound of tumbled stone and ran right into a sphinx.

Kennard jerked back and let out a surprised *meep* sound that made the others all stop and laugh.

"Where the hell are we?" Kennard asked.

"Cleopatra's Palace, Alexandria," Alec answered.

"Cleopatra?" Kennard cried. He pointed to his forehead. "The woman with a snake on her head? Have we not had enough of that for one day?"

Alec grinned at him, a bubble of air escaping his mouth

and floating upward. He pointed his thumb over his shoulder. "The next door is along here."

They swam farther along, and the way the moss and coral had covered the stone steps, the statues, it reminded Kennard of how the jungle had reclaimed the temples in Indonesia and Guatemala. Only underwater. The water was still, motionless, like the jungles had been when they'd gone through the split gates, like Alec's stop on time was still in effect.

Out of the depths came another structure. Stone, manmade, but covered in mollusks and coral, green seaweed and moss. It looked like a broken doorway, as though a doorway sat by itself absent walls or a roof, but Kennard recognized it for what it truly was. It was a split gate.

Alec, at the front and still holding Poseidon's trident, looked back at his friends. "Hold hands again," he said, and he disappeared through the doorway.

Again, the pressure changed, they were deeper down, the temperature was colder, and the water was murky. But Kennard could easily see the huge stone walls, intricate carvings, stone steps, and archways.

"This is Lion City in Shi Cheng, China," Alec said.

When he said city, he wasn't kidding. This place was huge. And one hundred feet under water. They started up the steps, swimming through an archway along a stone passageway that perhaps had once overlooked a courtyard, but now was the last step before the void of water.

Alec slowed and Kennard peered to see why, and he jerked back again when his eyes made out the shape through the murky water.

It was a stone carving of a Chinese sea dragon. It looked like Makara, only it was perched high up on the wall.

"It is only a statue," Alec said. "Come through here, it's not far now."

They each swam by the dragon statue, slowly, warily, not taking their eyes off it. It never moved, not like the stone statues had done in the jungle or even in the Golden Temple or in Atlantis. Kennard wondered if it was because their queen was dead. Manasa, the great basilisk, was dead. Maybe all her evil stone spawn were too.

Evil stone spawn? Alec asked in his mind.

What would you call them? He quipped back.

Alec laughed out loud. "Evil stone spawn works for me too." He followed a wall down some stairs and out to a stone courtyard with a split gate at the end. He turned and grinned at Eiji. "Eiji, this next one is for you, my friend."

They linked hands once more and slipped through the gate.

———

THIS TIME the water was incredibly blue, a little warmer, and there was much less pressure on Kennard's body. And the stone structure in front of them was huge, very old, and absolutely amazing.

The six of them trod water, looking up at it. Tiny in comparison.

"This is the Pyramid of Yonaguni-Jima, Japan," Alec said.

Eiji put his hand to his mouth in awe as he looked up at the tip of the pyramid. When he pulled his hand away, he was grinning. His long black hair fanned out behind him as he swam closer, reaching out to touch it. Jodis followed him, her hand on his back, and she kissed Eiji's cheek. Cronin followed and trod water beside Eiji as they looked up at the immense structure. The three of them had such a history. Eiji and Jodis had known Cronin for twice what Kennard had known him, and it was hard not to envy their closeness.

Me too, Alec said directly into Kennard's mind, obviously hearing his thoughts.

They're lucky, Kennard replied in his head.

Alec smiled and nodded. *They are. But we will have that too. Me with Cronin, you with Stas. You will have that too.*

Kennard turned to Stas. *Can you hear me?*

Yes, he replied with a smile. Kennard grinned and held out his hand, which Stas was quick to take. Stas lifted Kennard's hand to his lips and kissed his knuckles. *We will have history. Many years, yes?*

Kennard nodded. *Forever.*

Stas beamed, and Alec clapped Kennard on the shoulder before he swam over to the others.

Eiji turned to face him. "Thank you, Alec."

"You're very welcome," he replied, then he nodded to the right. "There's another gateway..."

They swam up the pyramid wall, huge stone blocks, perfectly squared but worn with time and water, and rounded the other side. There were more huge blocks, like steps for giants that would have perhaps been long walkways, and as they swam farther along, a wall came into view with three rectangular doorways.

"Hold hands," Alec said, and so they did, and he led them through to another underwater city.

The water was freezing; the pressure was harder on Kennard's head.

"Where is this?" Jodis asked, a grimace on her face.

"Lake Titicaca, Peru," Alec answered. "A sacred site for the Incas. According to Incan myth, the god Con-Tici Viracocha emerged from this lake with snakes for hair and holding serpents."

"I don't like it," Cronin said.

Kennard could have had a jibe at Cronin for being scared, but the truth was, he didn't like it either.

"Yeah. Let's find the next gate."

They swam in the frigid water, and the pressure felt as though it was squeezing Kennard's head. It was murky and dark but he could still make out the stone ruins. It reminded him oddly of Machu Picchu, only under water. After a short while, they found another wall with three identical matching doorways.

This is it, Alec said in his mind. *It feels like the last one, but I can't be sure.*

He held out his hand, which Cronin took, and they formed another chain. Alec gave them all a nod and he went through into the darkness.

Only when they came out the other side, they all fell into a wet and soggy heap on the floor of a jungle. Birds sang, wind soared through the trees, and somewhere in the distance monkeys were screeching. The humidity was oppressive, the shock of now being surrounded by air instead of water made them all cough. They got to their feet and pulled at their clothes, and Jodis and Eiji both peeled their long hair from their faces.

Kennard slipped his arm around Stas and turned around to look from where they had come. There was nothing there but the remains of a split gate, overgrown by the jungle, half-fallen and broken. Ruins of stone walls and snake carvings were being swallowed by the jungle.

Kennard took in the jungle surrounds, but nothing appeared to lurk or slither around them. "Alec, where the hell are we?"

"We're back in Indonesia. This is a lost Hindu temple." He squinted at the jungle. "I'm pretty sure this was once underwater."

"But we're back in the real world?" Eiji asked. "Real time?"

Alec gave a nod and looked skyward. "It will be morning soon. These trees won't give us enough protection from the sun."

"Then please," Kennard said. "For the love of Queen and country, take us back to London."

THE SIX OF them sat around Kennard's living room. Stas sat on the sofa, Kennard on the floor between his legs. On the opposite sofa, Cronin sat with his head lolled back and Alec sat on the floor between his legs. Jodis sat on a dining chair, her feet in Eiji's lap, and he was massaging her foot. The sun was rising over London, though no one seemed to care. No one spoke, no one moved. Still wet and muddy, they were all exhausted. Kennard didn't care about the state of the leather lounges or his pristine marble flooring. He didn't care at all.

Kennard lifted up one dirty socked foot. "I left my boots and jacket in the Golden Temple," he mumbled. "Shame. I liked those boots."

Alec gave a weary smirk. "We can go back and get them."

Kennard gave him a wry look. "I'd rather immigrate to Scotland."

Cronin lifted his head to stare at Kennard, slowly raised his hand, and gave Kennard the bird.

Eiji snorted out a laugh and Jodis smiled. "I haven't been this tired since I was human," she mumbled. "I think."

Was it all the swimming? Was it the traveling through all those gates? Was it traveling through the gates while time had stopped? Did that have an exponential effect on their bodies? Kennard didn't ask. Sure, vampires needed to sleep so being tired wasn't uncommon, but this was a different kind of weariness.

Perhaps it was now knowing all they'd learned. That there were such striking similarities between the ancient people of India and Asia, Japan, China, Mexico, Tibet, Egypt, the Greeks, and the Romans. How all those ancient civilizations had similar gods, myths, religions. They had similar architecture, pyramids, doorways, temples. They had carvings and drawings of the same creatures—snakes and sea serpents, dragons.

Vampires.

Each and every ancient society had instances of what historians believed were mass evacuations. But could it have been that ancient vampires, like Poseidon and Medusa, used these gateways to enter civilizations and feed on every last one of them? How else could they explain carvings from thousands of years ago of a creature with snakes for hair emerging from water in Peru and Greece and India?

It all made sense. Well, it didn't make any sense, really, Kennard allowed. At all. It was all so crazy and unbeliev-able, but he'd seen it with his own eyes.

Alec smiled at him. "If there's one thing I've learned, it's that history is never what it seems."

"It's fucked up, that's what it is," Kennard replied. He leaned his head against Stas' leg and Stas' fingers quickly raked through his hair. Kennard closed his eyes and began to purr.

"Speaking of fucked up," Cronin said. "Kennard? Is there something you'd like to share with us? Something about royalty and being a direct heir and rightful King of England, perhaps?"

Kennard sighed. "I'll tell you everything you want to know," he mumbled. He looked at Cronin then, meeting his eyes, and an understanding passed between them. For all the joking and jibes between them, they were dearest friends. "Perhaps it's a conversation for another day."

Cronin gave a nod. "Of course."

Kennard smiled and leaned his hand into Stas' touch, encouraging more scalp-scratching.

"I don't know about you guys," Eiji said. "But I could do with a feed."

Everyone nodded but no one made a move to get up or get changed.

"We don't have to go out, do we?" Jodis asked. "Can't we order in?"

Cronin chuckled. "What flavor do you feel like?"

"Hmm." Alec seemed to consider it for a moment.

"Uh, flavor?" Stas asked.

"What nationality of human," Kennard answered and Stas laughed a deep, rumbling sound.

But then Alec growled. "I feel like Chechen."

Normally when they 'ordered in' it was some disgusting prisoner from some obscure hellhole prison who had committed heinous crimes. The three men that suddenly appeared in Kennard's living room, bewildered and frightened, were disgusting and they had committed heinous crimes, that much was true. But they weren't prisoners.

They were politicians. Chechen politicians that Kennard recognized from the news on TV. The very so-called politicians who called for the genocide of LGBT people.

"Oh, Alec, you are a man after my own heart," Kennard said, smiling, his voice musical. He sprang to his feet and held one of the men by his jaw, who was now pale and sweating, paralyzed and stricken with fear.

The man was much taller than Kennard but no match. Not even close.

"You each deserve to die," Kennard said. He held the man up so his feet dangled and he thrashed futilely. Kennard knew his small frame and pretty face could turn frighteningly sinister when he wanted it to, and it quite often scared the literal life out of some humans. "I would do it quickly but you deserve to suffer. And you should know, you'll die by our very gay hands." The other two men fell backwards, trying to scamper away, but Alec and Jodis were quick to nab them. Stas leaned back in his seat and grinned, clearly proud of his man.

"Stas, my love," Kennard said. "Join me in our room." Stas didn't even need the visual of what Kennard wanted to do with him, to feed and to fuck, before he was on his feet and took their meal from Kennard and carried it to their room. Kennard turned to the others and grinned. "I won't apologize for all you're about to hear," he said with a laugh before he followed Stas and shut the door behind him.

Stas held the man out to him by the back of his neck. "You first, my Kennard," he said, his voice low and gruff. "I want to watch you feed."

Kennard walked slowly toward him, his gaze trained on Stas' eyes. He ignored how the human screamed and swore, kicked, and tried to pry Stas' hand from around his neck. Kennard licked his lips and extended his fangs. The man gasped and was now down to pleading for his life, but Kennard felt no remorse. Not for this piece of shit and the horrors he'd perpetrated.

Kennard pressed his teeth to the man's neck and sank his fangs into the jugular. He sucked and drank, and Stas' nostrils flared, his gaze growing dark. Kennard growled and purred as he pulled away so Stas could feed.

When they'd both had their fill and the man was drained, Stas simply let the body fall to the floor. He grabbed Kennard and pulled him close in a clash of bodies and mouths. Kennard's whole body thrummed with the rush of feeding and the heady feeling of anticipation. Stas was going to push all his buttons, fill him so completely, and wring pleasure from his bones.

Stas groaned into his mouth. "You think of such things..."

Kennard let his thoughts run back to every time they'd joined, every time they'd come, every ounce of pleasure. How it felt when Stas pushed into his body, how it felt when he pulsed and spilled inside him, how much pleasure he felt when Stas orgasmed.

The next thing Kennard knew, he was on his back on his bed and Stas was pressing him into the mattress. His face half an inch from Kennard's, his eyes dark, his breathing rough. "Your mind right now. You feel those things?"

"All of them," Kennard answered, smiling. "Now undress me and keep your mind on mine while you fuck me."

Stas' fangs extended and he growled. Kennard's clothes

were ripped from his body, and by the time Stas could prepare him, he was to the point of begging.

Stas, my love. I need you inside me. Your cock. All of it. Fill me with it and fuck me.

Stas' jeans disappeared, his huge cock hung hard, and he pushed against Kennard's tight body, into him, burying himself. Kennard cleared his mind of everything they'd done today, seen, learned, and admitted. He cleared it all away but the pleasure, the feeling of being taken, of being owned and loved. Stas pushed all the way in and Kennard wrapped his legs around him. Together they rocked, mouths and tongues searching, hands grasping, and bodies writhing... Kennard wanted Stas to experience this from his mind, and so he did. Several times. And when their bodies had had enough, Stas wrapped Kennard up in his strong arms, safe and sound, thoroughly sated, and they dozed.

ALEC AND CRONIN leapt into Kennard and Stas' London apartment living room. Kennard flitted over to them and kissed their cheeks. "Hello, my darlings."

Alec was holding something behind his back and quickly produced a pair of very fine Italian leather boots. Black and Versace. "To replace the ones you lost. I know they were your favorite."

Kennard let out a squeal, taking the boots. Of course, they had the Versace buckle. "They're beautiful. I could have done without the reminder."

"I thought the Medusa buckle was a nice touch," Alec said.

"True," Cronin added. "He thought it was funny."

Kennard chuckled, elated. "I can't believe you bought me new boots!"

"Well, *bought* is one way to put it," Alec grimaced. "More like leapt them from the factory."

Kennard sighed but decided he didn't care. The boots were gorgeous. "Well, it's the thought that counts. Thank you, darling."

"Anything for royalty," Cronin said. His smile and questioning gaze told Kennard he wasn't getting out of this.

Kennard resisted sighing but waved his hand toward where Stas was sitting on the sofa. "Take a seat."

Alec and Cronin sat on the sofa facing him. Kennard curled into Stas' side, tucked his legs up on the couch, and Stas was quick to hold Kennard's hand. He had, of course, divulged all to Stas already, and Alec could no doubt tell Cronin if he wanted to, but Kennard owed this to Cronin.

"What I said in Yakshi's temple was true. I was born in Westminster, to Edward IV, King of England, and his wife Elizabeth. I was older than my twin brother by only minutes, but it was he who would be king. *Should have* been king. I was hidden from public life, sickly and weak. I wasn't expected to survive, but I did. It was not to be made known that the king had offspring with failing health. It would make him, and England, appear weak." Kennard cleared his throat and Stas smiled at him, giving his hand an encouraging squeeze. It bolstered him to continue. "When my father died, my brother was crowned king. I remember quiet celebrations and I was happy for him. I wasn't jealous; I knew I couldn't do what was expected, and in a way, I was relieved. The dispute with the Lancasters had reached its peak with the death of my father."

"The dispute with the Lancasters?" Cronin asked incredulously. "You mean the War of the Roses?"

Kennard shrugged. "Yes. I remember much fuss being made about Edward being too young to take the crown, though I was kept hidden away. I spent most of my time with my younger brother and my sisters..." Kennard frowned and let out a long sigh. "Edward and I were twelve, merely children, when my... *uncle* became Lord Protector: legal ruler until Edward would become of age. We were taken to the Tower of London and..." Kennard raised his chin. "We were beaten, starved, tormented. My memories of that time are hazy. I became so ill and weak, I don't know if I was conscious or if my mind has chosen to spare me."

"I'm sorry you went through this," Cronin said sadly.

"So am I," Kennard said, affording him a small smile. "Perhaps it was my weak heart that saved me. Perhaps the vampire my uncle had sold us to thought me already dead. Perhaps he thought my blood poisoned or perhaps he'd already had his fill with my two brothers." Kennard frowned as the memories of their vacant eyes played in his head.

Stas could see the images in Kennard's mind and he leaned in and kissed the side of his head. Alec obviously saw it all too, and he flinched. "Kennard, I'm so sorry."

"He kept us alive for some time. Years. Who the bones they found hidden in the tower belonged to all those years later, I'll never know." Kennard shrugged. "Anyway, he actually experimented on bloodletting. He could influence behavior, so he would make my brothers compliant. They'd willingly offer their necks and wrists, but their eyes... I could see it. Glazed over but being fully aware." Kennard shuddered at the memory.

"Bloodletting?" Cronin asked.

"Yes. He would make incisions with blades and let the blood drain into cups," Kennard answered simply. "To drink, and to use in his experiments. Thinking he could keep human pets instead of killing so frequently. So people wouldn't become suspicious? I don't know."

"He hid you away?" Alec pressed on.

Kennard nodded. "In a basement under Suffolk Lane. It's gone now." He wiped the palm of his hand on his thigh. "Edward died first. We were seventeen..."

"He kept you for five years?" Cronin asked, his expression one of horror.

"Yes. The vampire who held us studied alchemy, of all things. He gave us different herbs and powders, but we'd not seen sunlight in years and my brothers grew ill. Edward gave Richard his food rations so that he might live, as did I. Richard was three years younger than us, but he was taller than me. I was smaller because of my heart..." Kennard smiled sadly. "Forgive me. My thoughts aren't as linear as they should be."

"It's fine," Cronin said gently.

Stas let go of Kennard's hand so he could put his arm around him instead.

"Anyway, my bastard uncle had died in battle three years prior apparently, and no one had missed the two princes. England had moved on, and a new king had brought years of peace." Kennard scowled. "Henry VII was a Welshman and a lord of fucking Ireland, of all places. As King of England! Yet I couldn't hold a grudge against him because he'd bested my uncle in battle. That bastard deserved a death more gruesome than to die defeated and alone on a muddy peat bog."

"The vampire who held you," Alec said. "What was his name?"

"Melchor," Kennard answered. "From Spain. Have I ever told you I don't much care for Spaniards?" he said with a smile. "Well, I don't. Melchor was almost a century old. He was strange, very eccentric, though with the luxury of hindsight, I can see he was a scientist."

"An alchemist," Alec corrected.

Kennard smiled. "Yes. He thought our blood was the answer to some great alchemical riddle. Our sangre azul, he used to call it. Our blue blood." He looked to Alec and smiled. "To obtain a blue flame that would burn hot enough to melt metal but be cold enough to hold in the palm of your hand. To create cohesion of the four elements, to create *alkahest*."

"The philosopher's stone," Alec said with a smile, his eyes wide.

Kennard nodded. "Who would have thought my two worlds would come full circle? My human life and my vampire life."

"You saved us in Atlantis," Alec said. "I couldn't do it. Only you could."

"Don't tell him that," Cronin said. "He'll get a fat head. The king's crown won't fit him... Wait," he said, a smile pulling at his lips. "Your father was Edward IV..."

Kennard sighed. He didn't need mind-reading abilities to know where this was going.

"He was French!" Cronin exclaimed. "Which means, you're part French!"

Kennard threw a cushion off the couch at Cronin's head. "Shut up. And you'll speak no more of it, or I'll claim my throne just to have you drawn and quartered. What was good for William Wallace..."

Cronin laughed and eventually Kennard did too. "I'm sorry you went through that," Cronin said sincerely. "And I'm sorry I never thought to press you for details on your human history."

"You did ask," Kennard said lightly. "I simply told you all I needed to. I never told anyone of my lineage."

"And this Melchor," Cronin asked. "What became of him?"

"He became complacent with us, with using his power to make us compliant, and Edward tried to escape to raise the alarm. Knowing he'd be recognized, Melchor became enraged and drained him where he stood. Then Richard tried to stop him, tried to fight him..." Kennard shrugged. "I was too weak. We all were. We were no match. He could have snapped us like twigs. He bit my neck, and given how weak I was, he must have assumed me dead. But I woke to the burning pain of change, feeling better and stronger than I *ever* had in my human life. The vampire bite saved me. I wasn't just better; I was cured. I knew enough from Melchor about what he was, how he fed, how he avoided sunlight, so I could survive without a sire's guidance. I ran across Melchor not long after and made him pay for what he did to my brothers." Then Kennard grinned. "And then, a few years later, I was having some fun with some humans in an alehouse, wagering some coin in a game of chance, when I happened to meet a redheaded vampire. A damned Scotsman, no less."

Cronin laughed. "And I thought to myself, this bloody English kid was trouble."

Kennard chuckled. "And the rest, as they say, is history."

"And none of your coven know?" Alec asked. "About your bloodline?"

"No. And I'd rather it stayed that way." Kennard took a deep breath. "I'm actually thinking of stepping down as coven leader. Given how things have changed," he said, smiling up at Stas.

Red Dirt Heart - L'intégrale (French translation of Red Dirt Series book set)

Rote Erde (German translation of Red Dirt Heart)

Rote Erde 2 (German translation of Red Dirt Heart 2)

Ein kleines bisschen Versuchung (German translation of The Weight of It All)

Ein kleines bisschen für immer (German translation of The Weight of It All Christmas)

65 Hours (Thai translation of Sixty Five Hours)

THANK YOU FOR READING

ALL REVIEWS ARE APPRECIATED

CRONIN'S KEY IV

KENNARD'S STORY

N.R. WALKER

History isn't always what it seems

CPSIA information can be obtained
at www.ICGtesting.com
Printed in the USA
LVHW041940220323
742311LV00004B/188